"That's it!" His patience, what there was of it, had been blown completely."

May eyed him mockingly now. "That's what, Mr. Marshall?" She smiled tauntingly.

"This!" he bit out forcefully—seconds before he swept her up into his arms and kissed that mocking smile right off her lips.

"Let go of me!" she ordered furiously, pushing ineffectually at his chest. She put up a hand to her slightly swollen lips, her eyes wide and accusing as she looked up at him. "I have no idea where you thought such behavior was going to get you. Get out," she told him quietly, shaking her head dazedly. "Just get out."

He gave her a deliberately mocking smile. "Don't feel too bad about responding, May," he said tauntingly. "You won't be the first woman to do so—or the last."

"Goodbye, Mr. Marshall."

Jude paused in the open doorway. "Oh, not goodbye, May," he assured her grimly. "Unlike my…associates, I don't intend leaving until I've done what I came here to do."

THE CALENDAR BRIDES

They've got a date—at the altar!

International bestselling author
Carole Mortimer has written more than
115 books, and now Harlequin Presents®
is proud to conclude her popular
CALENDAR BRIDES trilogy.

Meet the Calendar sisters:

January—is she too proud to become a wife?

March—can any man tame this free spirit?

May—will she meet her match?

These women are beautiful, proud and
spirited—and now they have three rich,
powerful and incredibly sexy tycoons ready
to claim them as their brides!

Available January, March and May 2004

Carole Mortimer

THE DESERVING MISTRESS

THE CALENDAR BRIDES

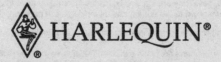
HARLEQUIN®

TORONTO • NEW YORK • LONDON
AMSTERDAM • PARIS • SYDNEY • HAMBURG
STOCKHOLM • ATHENS • TOKYO • MILAN • MADRID
PRAGUE • WARSAW • BUDAPEST • AUCKLAND

For Matthew—I'm so proud of you.

ISBN 0-373-12394-9

THE DESERVING MISTRESS

First North American Publication 2004.

CHAPTER ONE

'ARE you having a heart attack or just resting?'

May had heard the approach of the car into the farm-yard, had even managed to slightly raise one eyelid in order to register the fact that it wasn't a vehicle she recognised. Which meant her visitor was either lost, or a seed or fertilizer salesman, neither of which raised enough enthusiasm to rouse her from her sitting position on the convenient bale of hay outside the milking shed.

She managed a grunt of acknowledgement. 'Which do you think?'

'In all honesty—I'm not sure!' The man sounded slightly surprised by his own uncertainty, as if it weren't an emotion that came naturally to him.

May managed to pry that single eyelid slightly open a second time, just enough to be able to have a look at her unexpected visitor.

Probably aged in his mid to late thirties, the man was tall, very much so, with thick dark hair that looked inclined to curl, dark brows frowning over piercing grey eyes, an arrogant slash of a nose, his mouth grimly set over a squarely determined chin.

Uncertainty about anything certainly wouldn't sit easily on those broad shoulders, either!

'Well, let me know when you've made up your mind.' May sighed wearily, closing her eyelid again.

'Hmm,' he murmured thoughtfully. 'I've never actually seen anyone have a heart attack, but I'm sure they should be in more pain than you appear to be in. On the other hand, falling asleep sitting outside on a bale of hay, in a temperature that can't be much above freezing, doesn't seem too comfortable, either!' he concluded dryly.

May gave a dismissive movement of her shoulders. 'Anywhere is comfortable to fall asleep when you've been up all night.'

'Ah,' the man murmured knowingly.

She opened her eyes just wide enough to glare at him. 'With the vet,' she defended impatiently before closing her eyes again.

'I see,' the man drawled wryly.

May gave a groan as she roused herself to sit up on the bale of hay, every muscle in her body seeming to ache as she rubbed sleep-drowsed eyes before frowning up at her visitor.

When she viewed him more closely, it was possible to see the arrogant lift of his square-cut chin, the complete self-confidence in the way that he stood and the hardness of his handsome features. Just the type of man she felt like dealing with after a sleepless night!

'Can I help you?' she prompted irritably.

'That depends,' the man murmured ruefully.

'On what?' She sighed at this procrastination, really in no mood to deal with a lost out-of-season tourist or indeed a pushy salesman.

He shrugged those broad shoulders. 'On whether or not your name happens to be Calendar.'

Not a lost out-of-season tourist. A seed or fertilizer salesman, then.

'It could be.' She pushed herself up onto her feet with effort, looking up to find the man was still seven or eight inches taller than her own five feet eight in height.

The man gave her a considering look, laughter glinting in those piercing grey eyes now.

Which wasn't so surprising, May acknowledged, easily able to visualise the scarecrow figure she must represent. Her wellington boots were muddy, her jeans likewise; worse, she was still wearing the same clothes she had put on yesterday morning, not having been to bed yet or indeed managed to get inside for a refreshing shower. Her face was probably smeared with dirt from lying on the barn floor most of the night, a woollen hat pulled down low over her ears, mainly to keep out the bitingly cold wind but also to keep her long dark hair from the same muddy fate as the rest of her.

Yes, she had no doubts she did look rather funny. But at the moment, exhausted as she was, she wasn't in the mood to laugh, at herself or anyone else.

'You don't sound too sure,' the man drawled derisively.

'I'm not.' She shrugged, sighing heavily. 'Look, I have no idea what you're selling, and I probably don't want any anyway, but if you could come back tomorrow I might at least be willing to talk about it—'

'Selling?' he repeated frowningly. 'But I'm not the one—I have a better idea,' he stated briskly as May gave a weary yawn, at the same time swaying slightly on her feet. 'Let's go into the farmhouse.' He took a firm hold of her arm. 'I'll make you some coffee. Strong and black,' he decided after another glance at her face, her eyes appearing a deeper green against her paleness. 'And maybe then we can introduce ourselves properly.'

May wasn't sure she wanted to be introduced to this man, properly or otherwise, but the promise of making her coffee was certainly a strong inducement to at least letting him in as far as the kitchen. He probably made good coffee—he looked the sort of man who excelled at most things he did! And he didn't exactly look the type of man who felt the need to pounce on some unsuspecting female—in fact, with those looks, she suspected it was probably usually the other way round!

'Done!' she accepted huskily, allowing herself to be guided across the yard and into the kitchen, sitting down on one of the kitchen chairs as the man moved dexterously about the kitchen preparing a pot of strong coffee.

Lord, that smelt good, she acknowledged a few minutes later as the strong aroma of brewing coffee filled the warmth of the room. A cup or two might even help her to stay awake long enough to complete her chores for the morning.

It had been a long night, if ultimately a successful one, and the thought of all the jobs she still had to do had been the reason she'd sat down wearily on the bale of hay earlier. Only to fall asleep. Which, as this man had already pointed out, was not the most comfortable thing in the world to have done in late January.

'Here you are.' He placed a mug of strong black coffee in front of her before sitting down opposite her with another mug of his own, looking perfectly at ease in the confines of her untidy kitchen. 'I've added two sugars,' he told her frowningly. 'You look as if you need the energy.'

May didn't normally take sugar in her coffee, but she accepted that her visitor was right as she sipped the strong, sweet brew, instantly feeling the surge as the caffeine and sugar hit her bloodstream.

'I've made up my mind,' he murmured softly.

'Sorry?' May glanced across at him, frowning slightly. Obviously the caffeine and sugar hadn't done quite such a good job as she had thought—because she had no idea what he was talking about.

'You were sleeping earlier,' he stated firmly.

She grimaced. 'I already told you that I was.'

He nodded. 'Because you and the vet were up all night.'

When he put it like that...! 'With a ewe that was having a difficult time lambing,' she explained dryly. Not that it was any of this man's business, but still...

Their vet, John Potter, was a man of fifty or so, had been married for twenty years, and had three teenage children; it wouldn't do to have that sort of speculations spread around the neighbourhood. It wouldn't do her own reputation too much good, either!

'Mother and twins are all doing well,' she added dryly as this man continued to look at her with raised brows. 'Look, I'm grateful for the coffee and everything, but I really don't think I'm in any fit condition to—'

'Good Lord!' the man gasped suddenly.

'What...?' May was arrested in the action of removing her woollen hat, long dark hair cascading down over her shoulders and back.

He blinked, frowning darkly. 'You—I—for a moment— You reminded me of someone else.' He gave a dismissive shake of his head, but the dark frown remained on his scowling features. 'Who are you?' he breathed softly.

May gave him a scathing glance. 'Shouldn't I be the one asking you that? After all, I live here!' she reminded him impatiently.

'Yes. Yes, of course.' The man seemed to shake himself slightly, although his frowning gaze remained fixed on her face.

What on earth could he see there to have caused this

reaction? May wondered frowningly. With her long dark hair, deep green eyes, classical features, her looks were nothing exceptional. In fact, she had two younger sisters who looked very much the same as she did! Besides, dressed in her filthy clothing, her face probably covered in mud and goodness knew what else, she was hardly a glamorous figure. And this man, with his arrogant good looks and tailored clothes, did not look as if he usually bothered to look at mud-covered women farmers!

'Well?' she prompted irritatedly as he simply continued to stare.

'Well what…? Ah.' He shifted slightly in his chair as he obviously recalled her previous question, making no effort to answer her as his gaze roamed curiously around the kitchen, but mainly concentrating on the flagstone floor.

'What *are* you doing?' May finally demanded impatiently.

That piercing grey gaze returned to her face, this man seeming to have recovered from whatever had been bothering him about the way she looked. 'Looking for where you might have hidden the bodies, of course,' he drawled dryly.

Was she still asleep? Had her wonderful dream, where a handsome stranger appeared from nowhere and made her delicious coffee, turned into some sort of nightmare? Was she merely dreaming that she was sitting in her own kitchen, drinking coffee with a perfect stranger?

Because she certainly seemed to have lost the plot somewhere, this man's question making absolutely no sense to her!

Perhaps she wasn't dreaming. Perhaps this was all real. Perhaps this man was an escapee from a lunatic asylum!

'What bodies?' she prompted warily.

He was smiling when her gaze returned to his face, as if perfectly able to read her last, disturbing thought. 'Which one are you? May? March? Or January?' he prompted curiously.

Her wariness increased at his knowledge of her own name and those of her two sisters, too. An escapee from a lunatic asylum probably wouldn't know such things, but that didn't mean this man wasn't still dangerous.

'I'm May,' she answered brightly, forcing herself to an alertness she really didn't feel. 'But I'm expecting March and January back at any moment,' she lied.

One of her sisters was still in the Caribbean with her fiancé, and the other one had just gone to London with her fiancé to meet his family. But until she knew who this man was, and what he was doing here, she certainly didn't want him to know how completely alone she was here.

His mouth twisted into a humourless smile. 'Somehow I don't think so,' he murmured softly, that silver-grey gaze intent on the paleness of her face. 'So you're May,' he murmured consideringly.

'I just said so,' she confirmed defensively, shoulders tensed as she faced him across the table. 'And you are…?'

'I am.' He nodded unhelpfully, obviously enjoying her discomfort now.

May stood up forcefully, somehow feeling a little more in control of this situation once she was higher than he was—but at the same time knowing how quickly that would change if he were to stand up, too. 'Look, I didn't ask you here—'

'Ah, but you did,' he cut in softly, his voice almost a purr now, at the same time that his eyes glowed with challenge. 'In fact, I have it from two very reliable sources that you expressly wished to meet me face to face,' he assured her dismissively.

'I did?' May repeated slowly, suddenly becoming very still, looking at him with new eyes now, that mention of 'two very reliable sources' setting off alarm bells inside her head.

Mid to late thirties, very self-assured, obviously wealthy now that she took a good look at his leather jacket and designer-labelled jeans. More to the point, he had obviously already known she was one of the Calendar sisters when he arrived here.

Those alarm bells began to jingle so loudly they threatened to deafen her!

She knew who this man was—

'Jude Marshall,' he introduced confidently even as he stood up and held out his hand, knowing by the shocked look on her face seconds ago that the introduction was unnecessary.

Under other circumstances, that look of horror on her face at exactly who he was might possibly have been amusing. Possibly... Although he doubted it. It wasn't the usual reaction to his identity that he experienced from beautiful women. And May Calendar, despite her tired state, was an exceptionally beautiful woman.

She still stared at him, making no effort to shake the hand he held out to her. 'But—but—you're English!' she burst out accusingly.

Jude's hand dropped back to his side as he once again sat down on one of the chairs. 'Ah, now that is a debatable point,' he drawled, amused now by her stunned expression.

'Either you are or you aren't,' May Calendar snapped

dismissively, at the same time obviously making great efforts to regain her equilibrium after the shock of realising he was the man who had been trying to buy this farm for the last two months.

He shrugged. 'My mother is American, but my father is English,' he explained dryly. 'I was born in America, but educated in England. I visit America a lot, socially as well as on business, but my base is in London. So what do you think?' He quirked dark brows.

She gave him a resentful glare. 'I doubt you would want to hear what I think!'

'Probably not,' he drawled ruefully.

She was taking her coat off now, revealing that the bulky garment had hidden a curvaceous slenderness, her green jumper the exact colour of her eyes, denims fitting snugly over narrow thighs and long legs.

'Tell me,' Jude murmured softly. 'Do your sisters look anything like you?'

'Exac— Why do you want to know?' she amended her initial confirmation to a guarded wariness.

He shrugged. 'Just curious.'

'No, you weren't,' May Calendar said confidently. 'Those bodies you mentioned a few minutes ago, you wouldn't happen to be referring to Max Golding, your lawyer, and Will Davenport, your architect, would you?'

Bright as well as beautiful, Jude mentally conceded. The Calendar sisters—the one he had met so far, at least—were absolutely nothing like the three little old ladies he had assumed them to be several weeks ago when he'd first initiated the buying of their—this!— farm.

'What do you think?' he prompted unhelpfully.

'You're fond of answering a question with a question,

aren't you?' May murmured consideringly as she moved to refill her coffee mug.

It was a defence mechanism he had perfected over the years, meant that he usually obtained more information than he gave—and it wasn't something that most people easily recognised!

He frowned darkly. 'Obviously you share the same trait,' he bit out tersely.

She shrugged narrow shoulders. 'We could carry on like this all morning—except I don't have all morning to waste exchanging verbal arrows with you,' she added hardly.

'Because you and the vet spent a sleepless night together,' he came back with deliberate provocation.

Angry colour darkened her normally magnolia cheeks. 'I have already explained about that once, I don't intend doing so again!' she snapped dismissively. 'What is it you want, Mr Marshall?' she prompted challengingly.

Having now met the elder of the three Calendar sisters, found her to be absolutely nothing like he had presumed her to be, he wasn't absolutely sure. And that wasn't a feeling he was particularly comfortable with.

'Well, you might start off by telling me where Will and Max are?' he prompted cautiously.

'Assuming their bodies aren't hidden under the kitchen flagstones, after all?' she came back scathingly.

'Assuming that, yes,' he conceded with a humourless smile.

May Calendar gave a derisive shake of her head. 'They aren't.'

'Well?' he pushed impatiently a few seconds later when she added nothing to that remark.

She gave him a considering look, green eyes narrowed, her thoughts unreadable even to his experienced eye. 'Will is in London. Max is in the Caribbean,' she finally told him economically.

Jude drew in an impatient breath. 'And your two sisters are where?'

'March is in London. January is in the Caribbean,' she informed him with a challenging lift of her chin.

'How coincidental,' he drawled dryly.

In fact, he had already known exactly where Max and Will were, and who they were with; he had just wanted to see if May Calendar was willing to tell him as much. She obviously was!

'Not really—March and January naturally wanted to be with their fiancés,' she told him with satisfaction.

So Jude had gathered when he had received first a telephone call from Max over a week ago telling him of his engagement to January Calendar, and then a second telephone call from Will a couple of days ago telling him of his engagement to March Calendar!

To say he was surprised by the fact that his two friends were engaged to marry anyone, let alone two of the Calendar sisters, was an understatement.

The three men had been to school together, had worked together for years; despite relationships with numerous women over those years, Jude had always assumed that none of them would ever make the commitment to falling in love, let alone getting married. Obviously he had been wrong.

And that was something else he didn't admit to too freely!

He stood up abruptly. 'You asked me what I wanted a few minutes ago,' he rasped. 'I want exactly what Max was sent here to do before he fell in love with your sister, and that was to buy this farm!'

Her head tilted defensively. 'And I'm sure he's told you that it isn't for sale!'

Jude's eyes narrowed icily. 'Yes, he's told me.'

'And?'

The challenge was evident in her voice, as was the underlying tone of resentment. Both of which were going to get him precisely nowhere, Jude realised.

He forced himself to relax slightly, his smile lightly cajoling. 'May, surely you've realised, after the last few days of managing on your own here, that you just can't do it?'

She stiffened angrily, green eyes flashing with the emotion. 'What I can or cannot do is none of your business, Mr Marshall. And I don't remember giving you permission to call me by my first name, either,' she added churlishly.

He bit back the angry retort that sprang so readily to his lips, at the same time marvelling at the fact that this woman had managed to incite him to such an emotion. Usually he kept his emotions tightly under control, having found that this gave him an advantage over— Over what? His opponent, he had been going to say...

Was May Calendar really that?

Looking at her, tired from hard work and a sleepless night, her face ethereally lovely, much too slender than was healthy for her, it was difficult to think of her in that light. In fact, he was starting to feel guilty for having added to her obvious problems of the day.

Which was a highly dangerous direction for him to have taken!

'Look, maybe this isn't the best time for the two of us to talk,' he dismissed lightly. 'You're obviously busy, and tired, and—'

'And coming back tomorrow, when I might be neither

of those things, isn't going to change my answer one little bit,' she assured him scathingly. 'I'll tell you what I first told Max, your lawyer, and then Will, your architect—this farm is not for sale!'

Jude frowned at her frustratedly. She really was the most stubborn, intransigent—

'Certainly not to someone like you,' she continued insultingly. 'We don't need a health and country club where the Hanworth Estate used to be, Mr Marshall,' she scorned. 'Or the eighteen-hole golf course you intend to make of this farmland!'

She had done her homework, at least, Jude acknowledged admiringly—because that was exactly what he intended doing with this land once it was his. Unless, of course, Max or Will—

No! He didn't believe either man, no matter what his romantic connection with this family, would have betrayed the confidence he had in them. In fact, he knew that they hadn't, had already turned down Max's offer of resignation because of a 'conflict of interest', and viewed the two sets of plans Will had drawn up for this latest business venture, one including the Calendar farm, the other one not doing so.

He shrugged. 'That's only your personal opinion— Miss Calendar,' he added pointedly.

She shook her head. 'I believe, if you cared to ask around in the area, that you would find it's the general consensus of opinion, and not just mine.'

He didn't have time for this, Jude decided as he zipped up his jacket impatiently, better able to appreciate exactly what sort of brick wall Max and Will had come up against in their efforts to secure this farm for development. But May Calendar was going to find that he was made of much sterner stuff than either of his two

friends and work colleagues, that he wasn't so easily
distracted by a helpless female—or, indeed, three of
them!

'We'll talk about this some other time, Miss
Calendar,' he dismissed uninterestedly, pausing at the
door to add, 'It's enough for now that we have introduced ourselves to each other.' And that she now knew
what sort of opposition she was up against.

Because Jude had no intention of giving up on his
plans for the property he had already bought in this area,
plans that included the Calendar sisters' farm.

No intention whatsoever!

CHAPTER TWO

WELL, that was certainly a turn-up for the book, May acknowledged as she dropped down weakly onto one of the kitchen chairs after Jude Marshall's abrupt departure.

He was the very last person she had expected to see today—or, indeed, at any other time.

Jude Marshall, and the corporation that he headed, had become something of an elusive spectre in the background of the sisters' lives the last couple of months, ever since they had received a letter from that corporation with an offer to buy their farm. A farm that, as far as any of the Calendar sisters was concerned, had never been for sale.

That initial letter had come from America, which was why they had all assumed that Jude Marshall was American, too—and why, when he'd spoken in that precise English accent on his arrival a short time ago, May had made absolutely no connection between her unexpected visitor and the man whose very name the three sisters had all come to loathe the last two months.

Jude Marshall was a surprise in more ways than one, May acknowledged frowningly. She hadn't expected him to be so arrogantly good-looking, for one thing, or have him moving capably about her kitchen making her a much-needed mug of coffee, for that matter!

He was also, she acknowledged less readily, completely right about the strain of running the farm on her own the last few days since her sister March had gone off to London to meet Will's parents, and her younger sister January had telephoned from the Caribbean to say that she and Max had decided to stay on for an extra week. January had sounded so happy and carefree that May hadn't liked to tell her youngest sister that, with March away, too, she was managing here on her own, brightly assuring January that everything was just fine here, and wishing her and Max a wonderful time.

Something she certainly wasn't having herself!

This last few days on her own had been a learning experience, was indicative of how it would be once March and January were married and living away from the farm. Not good, May knew.

But that was still no reason to give in to Jude Marshall's pressure to sell the farm to him, she decided with a determined straightening of her spine. Having now met the man, and seeing firsthand just how arrogantly assured he was, May was even more determined not to do that!

Although she didn't feel quite so confident later that evening when she staggered back into the farmhouse, too tired to even bother to cook herself an evening meal.

The coffee remaining in the pot from this morning was stewed and only lukewarm, but it was better than nothing.

No, it wasn't, she decided after the first mouthful, putting the mug back down on the table with a disgusted grimace.

She was so tired, so utterly exhausted, resting her head down on her folded arms as she sagged tiredly onto the kitchen table. Just a few minutes' rest and she would be all right again, she told herself. Just a few minutes…

'Come on, May, it's time to wake up,' a gently intruding voice cajoled. 'May?' A gentle shaking of her arm accompanied this second intrusion.

She had been having such a nice dream, she frowned resentfully, had been lying on a golden beach, the sun warm and soothing, with a tropical blue sea lapping lightly against the sand at her feet. But the stiffness in her folded arms as she slowly woke to consciousness, aided by the ache in her back, told her only too clearly that it had unfortunately been just a dream!

'May, if you don't wake up in a minute, I'm going to assume that this time you really have had a heart attack—and commence emergency mouth-to-mouth resuscitation!' that intruding voice drawled mockingly.

Jude Marshall's voice!

She recognised those clipped English tones only too easily this time, raising her head to glare at him resentfully, very aware that she probably looked worse now than she had this morning, still in the same clothes, still as dirty—and, to add to her disarray, she probably had crease marks on her face now from having fallen asleep in such an uncomfortable position!

He grinned down at her unconcernedly. 'I thought the mere suggestion of my having to carry out mouth-to-mouth resuscitation might revive you!'

She gave an irritated sigh. 'What do you want, Mr Marshall?'

'You seem very fond of asking me that.' He raised mocking brows. 'A fine way to talk to someone who has brought you dinner,' he admonished derisively, holding up a plastic carrier bag. 'Chinese take-away,' he explained economically. 'Having seen how tired you were this morning, I didn't think you were going to be in any fit state to cook yourself a hot meal this evening.'

May frowned up at him, still not quite awake, but aware enough to view his kindness—and the man himself!—with suspicion. The fact that his surmise had obviously been a correct one wasn't in question—but his response to it certainly was.

'And why should that bother you, Mr Marshall?' she prompted warily, her sleepy state fast disappearing now as she frowned up at him suspiciously.

'Stop dithering, woman, and tell me where the plates are so that I can serve this stuff before it goes cold!' He put the bag down on the table in front of her.

'Second cupboard on the right,' she supplied somewhat dazedly. Plates, he had said. In the plural. Surely this man didn't intend sitting down to dinner with her?

But as he set out two places on the table along with the two big plates, and then commenced to put out the cartons of Chinese food, it appeared that was exactly what he intended doing!

'Er—Mr Marshall—'

'Could we get something clear right now, May?' He straightened, looking down at her with narrowed eyes.

She stiffened warily, wondering exactly what he was going to say. 'Yes?'

He nodded abruptly. 'I'm sure you have your reasons for being deliberately rude to me—I'm sure you *think* you have,' he stressed firmly as she would have protested. 'But I have no intention of sitting down to dinner—a dinner that I actually brought here, remember?—with someone who insists on calling me ''Mr Marshall'' in that unfriendly tone.' He raised dark brows pointedly.

May's cheeks warmed at the accusation. She was being deliberately rude, there was no denying that. But he was being deliberately friendly, which was just as unacceptable!

'Okay?' he prompted determinedly.

May looked up at him unblinkingly, wanting to tell him to go away, and to take his dinner with him. But the smell of the food was so tempting, her mouth watering at the mixture of aromas that was wafting up from the array of cartons he had put out in the middle of the table. If she told him to go away, he would probably take all this wonderful food with him!

'Okay,' she accepted abruptly. 'Although—'

'Okay will do for just now,' Jude cut in derisively. 'Eat,' he added curtly, sitting down at the place opposite her.

She couldn't remember the last time someone had ordered her about in this way. Probably not since her father had died a year ago, she recognised frowningly. But anyone less like her father—or, indeed, a father-figure—than Jude Marshall, she was less likely to meet!

For one thing she was completely aware of him as the two of them helped themselves to the food, of the slender strength of his ringless hands, the dark hairs that began at his wrist and probably covered his arms and chest, of the way his dark hair fell endearingly across his forehead unless pushed back by an impatient hand, of the piercing intelligence of those silver-grey eyes, of the dark shadow at his jaw that implied he probably had to shave twice a day, but had omitted to spend time on that second shave today.

Because he had chosen to drive out here and bring her dinner instead? Probably, she acknowledged slightly dazedly. In fact, she found it difficult to believe at all that she was sitting here eating a Chinese take-away with Jude Marshall, of all people!

'This is very good, thank you,' she told him huskily, the hot, tasty food more welcome than she had even imagined. And it had been supplied by Jude Marshall, a man she considered to be her enemy...

He looked across at her, eyes gleaming silver with

amusement. 'How hard was that to say?' he mused dryly.

'Very,' she confirmed with a rueful grimace. 'I hope I'm not keeping you from something? Or someone?' she added frowningly.

'Nothing that can't wait.' He shrugged dismissively.

May gave him a quizzical look. Did that mean there wasn't someone waiting for him back at his hotel? Or that the person that was waiting for him wasn't important enough for him to bother rushing back to?

Jude frowned as he saw her looking at him. 'What did I say now?' he prompted impatiently.

'Nothing,' she dismissed abruptly, deliberately turning her attention back to her food.

Although she was completely aware of the fact that he was still looking at her. If she was honest—and she usually was—she had to admit she had never been so aware of another person in her life before.

Just as she felt sorry for whoever—possibly?—might be waiting for him back at his hotel; it would be awful to be so unimportant to this man that his having dinner with a scruffy female farmer took priority. Even with the buying of this farm as the incentive.

'I spoke to Max earlier this evening.'

May looked up at him sharply, but his bland expression was completely unenlightening. She moistened her lips before speaking, choosing her words carefully, deliberately infusing a lightness into her tone. 'Did you tell him the two of us have met—finally?' she couldn't resist adding dryly.

Jude sat back, regarding her derisively. 'Should I have done?' he drawled.

He was doing it again—answering a question with a question.

Because he knew damn well that she would much rather Max, and consequently January, didn't know of his presence in the area, or that he had already introduced himself to her—but especially that she was managing alone here on the farm.

January had had a pretty awful time of things at the beginning of the year, had been caught up in the sick workings of a stalker's mind, May much relieved when her sister had become engaged to Max, even more pleased when he'd suggested taking her away for a few weeks' holiday to get over the experience.

But she had no doubts that, were January to learn of Jude Marshall's presence here, of the fact that May was alone on the farm, her sister would insist on coming back on the next available flight!

'Well?' she prompted impatiently.

Jude gave a rueful shake of his head as she neatly turned the tables back on him. 'You're right—we could go on like this all night, returning a question with a question!'

'Not all night, no,' May assured him scathingly. 'Tonight I intend going to bed early, very early—and alone,' she added so that there should be no more mistakes concerning that particular subject! 'In fact—' She broke off frowningly as a knock sounded on the door, shooting Jude Marshall an accusing look.

'January would hardly knock to come into her own home,' he easily read the accusation in that look—and the reason for it.

Which still didn't tell her whether or not he had mentioned to Max that he had decided to come here himself as he and Will had failed to acquire the Calendar farm for him. But, then, even on this short an acquaintance, May already knew that Jude Marshall was decidedly economical in providing any sort of information about anything.

May stood up as a second knock sounded on the door. 'We'll talk on this subject more once I've dealt with my visitor,' she warned before moving hurriedly to the door, intending to make it very clear to this man before he left this evening that January was not to be worried by the situation here.

And 'situation' it certainly was rapidly becoming, she decided dazedly as she opened the door to find David Melton standing on her doorstep.

Keen on amateur dramatics, May had joined the local society a couple of years ago, only to be spotted by David Melton, a renowned film director, when he'd come to visit his sister's family for Christmas and spotted May as she'd performed in the local pantomime.

To her surprise he had offered her a part in the film he was to shoot in the summer, if the screen test he offered proved to be successful. It had. But, for very personal reasons of her own, May had decided to turn down his offer...

Which was why she had no idea what he was doing standing on her doorstep now.

Jude watched May's face as she obviously recognised her visitor—but obviously wished that she didn't, her expression a puzzling mixture of surprise and dismay.

He turned his narrowed gaze on the other man; probably aged forty or so, tall and slender, with short blond hair and a boyishly handsome face. Which told him precisely nothing, Jude acknowledged ruefully. The man could just be a salesman or something equally innocuous—although, from May's reaction to seeing him, somehow Jude doubted it...

'David,' he heard May greet huskily.

'I was in the area—I had to come, May,' the man returned determinedly.

May shook her head. 'I haven't changed my mind,' she told him firmly.

'But—'

'You'll find someone else,' she assured him, an uncomfortable glance in Jude's direction letting the other man know that she wasn't alone.

David shot Jude an impatient glance of his own before his attention returned determinedly to May. 'I don't want anyone else, May,' he told her forcefully. 'It has to be you. You're perfect—'

'I really don't want to talk about this just now,' May cut in firmly, obviously completely conscious of the listening Jude, even if the other man seemed unconcerned by his presence.

Curiouser and curiouser, Jude acknowledged consideringly. Was this David a spurned lover who simply refused to go away? Or something else? Although quite what that 'something else' could be Jude had no idea. Which brought him back to the spurned lover theory… Although, in the other man's shoes, Jude would have been more than a little concerned at another man's presence here alone with May. Unless the other man considered him to be insignificant in what was going on between him and May? A thought that Jude, who had never thought of himself as in the least 'insignificant' in any situation, found intensely irritating.

He stood up, moving to stand at May's side, deliberately resting his hand on the door behind her. 'Is there a problem, May?' he prompted haughtily.

She shot him a frowning glance. 'Nothing that I can't handle. Thank you,' she added belatedly.

Jude turned his attention on the other man, deliberately looking down the long length of his nose, topping the other man by at least three inches. 'I'm afraid you've caught us right in the middle of eating our dinner...' he said pointedly.

The other man looked displeased at this interruption. 'I just wanted to have a few words with May—'

'And, as I've just told you, we're eating our evening meal,' Jude bit out with hard dismissal, his gaze challenging on the other man now.

May looked up at him frowningly, seeming to sense that the situation was fast moving out of her control, turning back to David smilingly. 'I appreciate your— continued interest,' she told him warmly. 'But, as I told you before, I'm really not interested.'

David shook his head. 'I'm not giving up.'

May looked completely baffled as to what to do or say next to this man, shaking her head dazedly.

'I don't understand what went wrong,' David continued forcefully. 'One minute you were fine with everything that we had talked about, the plans we had made, and the next—'

'How many times does she have to tell you she's not interested?' Jude cut in coldly, stepping forward slightly to drape a proprietorial arm about May's narrow shoulders. Too narrow, he realised frowningly. She really was too thin, too delicate, to live the hard-working life that she so obviously did.

David's gaze became guarded as he looked at that possessive arm about her shoulders. 'And you would be...?' he prompted slowly.

'I would be a friend of May's,' Jude answered harshly.

'I see,' the other man murmured, obviously not seeing at all as he turned to look questioningly at May.

'I would really much rather not talk about this any more, David,' she told him regretfully. 'I-it was a nice dream while it lasted,' she added wistfully. 'But it really isn't for me. I'm sorry.' She grimaced.

Her visitor drew in a ragged breath, hunching his shoulders as he thrust his hands into the pockets of his sheepskin jacket. 'I'm not giving up,' he assured her decisively. 'I'll be back.' He nodded firmly. 'Perhaps we can talk then.'

'I wouldn't count on it,' Jude put in raspingly, his patience wearing very thin where this man was concerned. Couldn't he see, and just accept, that May wasn't interested? That she wanted him to leave and not come back to bother her?

Was this how Max and Will had felt, too? he wondered a little dazedly; protective, but at the same time finding their Calendar woman incredibly attractive?

Except that May Calendar was not his woman. Would never be his woman. Not if he had anything to say about it. And he most certainly did.

'Are you staying with your sister again?' May was talking to the other man again now. 'I'll ring you there some time tomorrow,' she added quickly as she received confirmation of that fact with David's nod.

'I'll be waiting for your call,' he assured her huskily before turning his hard blue gaze on Jude. 'Goodnight,' he added coldly.

'Goodbye,' Jude returned with a challenging lift of his dark brows.

The other man gave a humourless smile of acknowledgement at the obviously male challenge before turning to walk across to his car, a sporty Jaguar, Jude noted with displeasure; obviously this David, whoever he was, was wealthy enough to help May if he wanted to. And, from their conversation, he obviously did.

And yet she seemed uninterested in whatever the other man had to offer, so perhaps—

'And just what the hell did you think you were doing just now?' May's angry challenge was accompanied by the slamming of the door as she turned to face him, her cheeks fiery red with anger, her eyes glittering deeply green.

He raised mocking brows at the unexpected attack. 'Trying to be helpful?' he prompted pointedly. 'The man was obviously bothering you, and so I—'

'Helpful? Helpful?' she repeated incredulously, hands clenched at her sides. 'Can you drive a tractor?'

He blinked frowningly. 'Unfortunately not.'

'Milk a cow?'

He grimaced. 'Definitely not!'

'Nurse a weak lamb?'

He shrugged. 'Probably not.'

'Feed the hens and collect the eggs?'

He drew in an impatient breath, knowing exactly where this conversation was going. 'Look, May—'

'No, of course you can't do any of those things!' she answered her own questions impatiently. 'But I can, and I do. And *those* are the only ways that you could possibly be of any help to me, Mr Marshall,' she told him scathingly. 'I really don't know where you got the impression that I'm some helpless female that needs rescuing—'

'Don't you?' he rasped pointedly.

She had the grace to blush, her exhausted condition earlier having been unmistakable. 'That was an exceptional circumstance,' she dismissed firmly. 'Now, if you wouldn't mind leaving...?' She stood pointedly away from the door, her expression challenging.

Jude gazed at her frustratedly. She really was the most—

Were those tears he could see in those incredible green eyes? And if so, were they tears of sheer frustration with all the work she had to do, or were they for some other reason?

'We haven't finished our meal,' he pointed out softly.

She gave a shake of her head. 'I'm afraid I've completely lost my appetite.'

'May—'

'Will you just go?' she cried emotionally, the tears welling against the darkness of her lashes now.

'No—I won't just go,' he answered impatiently. 'May, I don't think for one minute that you're a helpless female.' How could he, when she had obviously been the female mainstay of this household since she was nothing but a child herself? 'But you are wrecked, anyone can see that from just looking at you—'

'Thanks!' she snapped scathingly.

He sighed heavily. 'There's just no reasoning with you, is there?'

'None at all,' she bit out coldly.

Jude shook his head. He had never met a woman like May Calendar before. Had never felt like shaking and kissing a woman at the same time before, either—

Kissing...?

Damn it, yes, he wanted to kiss May Calendar! Wanted to sweep her up into his arms and kiss her until she was senseless. Until they were both senseless.

Which was why he most certainly wasn't going to do it!

'Fine,' he rasped harshly, picking up his jacket from

the back of the chair before walking determinedly to the door. 'Any message for Max or your sister if he should happen to telephone again?' he challenged hardly, already knowing from her reaction earlier to his casual mention of having spoken to Max that she did not want her youngest sister to know she was coping alone here.

She swallowed hard, her cheeks suddenly pale now. 'No—' she moistened dry lips '—no message. Except—'

'Yes?' He paused at the door.

She gave the ghost of a smile. 'You could tell January that Ginny and the twins are all doing well. The ewe from last night, and her two lambs,' she explained ruefully at his puzzled frown.

Jude gave an acknowledging inclination of his head, not having particularly enjoyed scoring that point, where Max and January were concerned, over a woman who was so exhausted she could hardly see straight. 'I would get that early night if I were you, May—before you fall over!' he rasped.

She gave a shake of her head. 'I still have things to do.'

He gave an impatient shrug at her stubbornness. 'Your choice,' he bit out harshly. 'But, from the look of things, they will still be there for you to do all over again tomorrow.'

She gave the hint of a smile. 'My father used to say that.'

Used to. Because, as Jude now knew only too well, having checked up on the Calendar sisters a little more thoroughly after Max had got himself engaged to one of them, neither of the Calendar parents were still alive, the mother having died while the three girls were still very young, the father only a year ago.

Which really made him feel good about trying to buy the farm out from under them!

'Then you should have listened to him!' he rasped, no longer sure whether it was May or himself that he was angry with.

One thing he did know, he needed to get this whole thing back into perspective, to concentrate on his objective, which was to buy this land and then leave.

And, to do that, he had to get away from May Calendar.

Besides, April would be waiting for him back at the hotel. Charming, entertaining, thoroughly agreeable April.

May Calendar looked at him unblinkingly. 'I did listen to him, Mr Marshall, but I don't have to listen to you—'

'That's it!' His patience, what there was of it, had been blown completely at her determined continuation of the formal 'Mr Marshall'. Damn it, he had tried to be kind to her—even though she would so obviously have preferred that he wasn't—to be reasonable; he had even bought her dinner.

With no ulterior motive? a little voice taunted inside his head.

And what if there had been? She could still have been a little more grateful than she had.

May eyed him mockingly now. 'That's what, Mr Marshall?' She smiled tauntingly.

'This,' he bit out forcefully—seconds before he swept her up into his arms and kissed that mocking smile right off her lips.

Mistake, Jude, he admitted with an inward groan. Mistake!

She tasted of honey. Her lips were soft and responsive—probably because she was too surprised to do anything else, he acknowledged ruefully, even as he moulded her body against his, the warmth of her breasts crushed against his chest, the dark swathe of her silky hair falling down over his arm as he tilted her head back to deepen the kiss.

Nectar.

Sweet, sweet, nectar.

So intent was he on tasting that nectar that he didn't at first notice the tiny fists pummelling against his chest, only coming to a full awareness of her resistance as she wrenched her lips away from his to glare up at him.

'Let go of me,' she ordered furiously, pushing ineffectually at his chest now. 'You—you—'

'Yes?' he derided challengingly even as his arms dropped back to his sides and he stepped away from her.

It had taken several seconds to get his own raging emotions back under control, but now that he had…

Exactly what had he thought he was doing? Okay, so May was beautiful, immensely desirable, challenging— but she was also, in this particular situation, the opposition!

She put up a hand to her slightly swollen lips, her eyes wide and accusing as she looked up at him. 'I have no idea where you thought such behaviour was going to get you, but… Get out,' she told him quietly, shaking her head dazedly. 'Just get out.'

Oh, he was going, intended putting as much distance between himself and this woman as possible.

She was dangerous. To his self-control. To his self-preservation. To his self-possessed existence!

He gave her a deliberately mocking smile. 'Don't feel too bad about responding, May,' he said tauntingly. 'You won't be the first woman to do so—or the last,' he added derisively.

If anything her face paled even more, those glittering green eyes the only colour in her face now. 'Get out!' she repeated between clenched teeth.

Jude calmly bent to pick up the jacket he had dropped seconds ago to take her into his arms, easily holding her accusing gaze as he put the jacket on, deliberately taking his time, much to her obvious impatience.

'Have something else to eat, May,' he drawled as he walked to the door. 'It would be a pity to waste all that food just because you don't like the person who bought it for you,' he added dryly.

'Goodbye, Mr Marshall,' she said as pointedly as he had to the man called David a few minutes ago.

Jude paused in the open doorway. 'Oh, not goodbye, May,' he assured her grimly. 'Unlike my—associates, I don't intend leaving until I've done what I came here to do.'

She gave a scornful laugh. 'Then I would suggest you start looking to buy a house in the area—because I'm not interested in selling the farm, to you or anyone else.'

'No, you're obviously not,' he accepted lightly. 'But your sisters may feel differently now that they are both engaged to be married.'

Jude regretted having made this last challenge even as he made it. He saw the way her cheeks paled once again, that slightly haunted look in those deep green eyes telling him that she was no longer as sure of her sisters' feelings in the matter as she wanted him to think she was.

Making him feel like a complete heel.

Oh, he was determined, forceful, had never let a business challenge get the better of him, but he had never considered himself to be deliberately cruel before.

What the hell was wrong with him?

May Calendar, with her big green eyes, her magnolia skin, her air of fragility, that was what was wrong with him.

And it stopped right now!

'Have a nice day,' he told her glibly, closing the door softly behind him before strolling over to get back into his hire car.

Damn, damn, *damn*!

CHAPTER THREE

'THIS is very kind of you, David.' May smiled shyly across at him as they sat in the bar of the hotel restaurant while waiting to go to their table. 'But I'm afraid it's just a waste of your time, that it isn't going to change anything,' she added with a rueful shake of her head.

'I don't consider having dinner with a beautiful woman as time wasted,' David Melton assured her huskily, blue gaze warm in the rugged handsomeness of his face.

He was so nice; that was what made all of this so difficult. That, and the fact that May really would have loved to accept the part in his forthcoming film he had repeatedly offered her. But, for reasons she had no intention of telling him—or, indeed, anyone else—the whole thing was simply impossible.

But she had kept her promise to telephone David at his sister's earlier today, had repeated what she had told him in London a couple of weeks ago, and again yesterday evening, only to have him ask her to come out to dinner with him this evening. No pressure, he had assured her as she'd hesitated, just a friendly dinner together, when he wouldn't even mention the film role if she would rather he didn't.

It had been too tempting an offer for her to refuse, David extremely handsome as well as being a charmingly interesting man. And with the added incentive not to mention the film role...

And now she had been the one to introduce the subject…!

Primarily because she felt so guilty about the time David had taken to give her the screen test a couple of weeks ago—only to have her turn down his offer after that test had proved successful.

To be offered a film role, on the basis of one performance in a local pantomime, was the stuff that actresses' dreams were made of, and May knew that David must wonder at her sanity for having turned down such an offer.

'Does your reluctance concerning playing the role of Stella have anything to do with the man I met last night?' David prompted lightly, looking at her over the top of his glass as he took a sip of the white wine he had ordered for them both as a pre-dinner drink.

'The man you— Oh.' May grimaced as she realised exactly whom he was talking about. 'No,' she assured him with a firm shake of her head. 'Jude is a total irrelevance to this situation— What's so funny?' she prompted with a puzzled frown as he gave a husky chuckle.

He gave a rueful shake of his head. 'I doubt that particular man has ever considered himself an irrelevance in any situation!' he explained dryly.

May smiled at what she was sure was an accurate observation where Jude Marshall was concerned. 'No, I'm sure that he hasn't,' she agreed. 'But in this case, he is,' she insisted firmly.

David gave her a puzzled glance. 'Who is he, exactly?'

She knew what he was—exactly! Jude Marshall was a sneaky opportunist, a man who had taken advantage of her extreme tiredness the evening before; more importantly—he was trying to buy their farm out from under them.

'No one of any importance,' she dismissed hardly, remembering all too clearly that Jude had kissed her yesterday evening. Worse—she remembered that she had kissed him back.

She had been too surprised initially to do anything but stand in shocked immobility in Jude's arms, but, once the shock had worn off, instead of pushing him away, as she should have done, she had responded. That was something she wasn't about to forgive him for in a hurry!

'I'm glad to hear it.' But David still didn't look totally convinced by her dismissal of Jude.

Time to change the subject, May decided—in fact, it was past time! 'Are you staying in the area long?'

David shrugged. 'Another couple of days or so, I think. May—' he sat forward, his gaze suddenly intense '—there's someone I would like you to meet while I'm here.'

Her eyes widened. 'There is?' As far as she was aware, the only people that David knew in the area were her and his sister's family, and surely he didn't want to introduce her to them?

She found him good company, had enjoyed the time they'd spent together when she'd gone to London for her screen test a couple of weeks ago, but this was the first time the two of them had gone out on anything resembling a social basis...

'Yes.' He was still watching her intently. 'You see—'

'Well, well, well, so you don't spend *all* your time milking cows and feeding hens, after all,' an all-too-familiar voice drawled mockingly.

May closed her eyes briefly, taking a deep breath before answering; Jude Marshall was positively the last person she had wanted to meet this evening. Well... maybe not the last person, she conceded frowningly, but he came pretty close.

'Mr Marshall,' she greeted wearily, deliberately keeping her expression noncommittal as she looked up at him.

Which wasn't easy when he looked so devastatingly attractive!

She had thought David handsome in his dark suit and blue shirt when they'd met in the foyer of the hotel earlier, but Jude Marshall in a dinner suit was something else; his shoulders were wide, his waist tapered, his legs long and lean, the snowy white of his shirt emphasising the golden tan of his face and hands, those grey eyes appearing almost silver against that tanned skin.

May straightened determinedly. She was not going to sit here like some gauche schoolgirl overwhelmed by a handsome, sophisticated man. Even if that was how she felt...

'Or wearing wellington boots and woollen hats,' she returned dismissively, knowing that she at least looked presentable this evening.

Jude's gaze swept assessingly over her appearance, grey eyes narrowed as he took in her newly washed hair as it swayed silkily over her shoulders, her dark green dress shimmering against her slender curves to reveal the silky length of her legs.

His gaze returned deliberately to her face. 'Obviously not,' he drawled before turning slowly to look at the man who sat with her. 'I don't believe we've been introduced...?' He raised dark brows pointedly.

Other than behaving as rudely to Jude as he had to

him the previous evening, May knew that David had no choice but to stand up and introduce himself.

'David Melton.' He held out his hand politely.

'Jude Marshall,' Jude returned as economically, an edge of mockery to his voice as he looked at the other man assessingly. 'Melton…?' he repeated slowly. 'Now where have I—?'

'I believe our table is ready, David,' May cut in force-fully even as she rose gracefully to her feet, having no-ticed the waiter hovering around in the background try-ing to attract their attention. 'If you'll excuse us, Jude…' she added decisively, green gaze challenging on his.

He returned that gaze steadily for several long sec-onds, and then his gaze slowly dropped down the slender length of her body. By the time his gaze returned to her face, May could feel the heated wings of colour in her cheeks.

As well as a slight trembling of her limbs, and a short-ness of breath, as if she had been running…

'You're dining at the hotel?' he prompted sharply.

May suffered a sinking feeling in the pit of her stom-ach. It had never occurred to her, when David had asked her to join him here for dinner, that, being the best hotel in the area, this was probably the hotel Jude Marshall was staying at. But it occurred to her now.

It also occurred to her, from the way he was dressed, that Jude Marshall was dining here, too. And not alone, if the formality of the dinner suit was anything to go by.

'Obviously.' She eyed him challengingly. 'And you?'

'Obviously,' he returned dryly. 'I'm just waiting for my dining companion,' he confirmed lazily. 'Perhaps the four of us could get together for a drink after we've eaten?' Dark brows rose challengingly over those mock-ing grey eyes.

And perhaps they couldn't! She was here with David, and it was pretty obvious that Jude's dining companion was going to be a beautiful woman; the last thing she wanted was to sit and have a drink with the pair of them at the end of the evening. It would probably choke her.

'I don't think so—thank you,' she added belatedly. 'Some of us have to get up early in the morning,' she added pointedly.

'Thanks for the offer, anyway,' David cut in cheerfully before the other man could come back with the cutting reply that was obviously hovering on those sculptured lips, David taking a firm hold of May's arm as they turned to follow the waiter into the dining-room.

And May could feel that icy grey gaze following them every step of the way.

Her breath left her in a heavy sigh as she sat down at the table, the first indication that she had of having held it in, her legs feeling slightly shaky, too. But Jude Marshall had that effect on her, she acknowledged heavily; she seemed to want to either hit him or kiss him at any given moment—and just now the former had definitely won out.

'I'm really sorry about that.' She gave David a rueful smile. 'I'm starting to feel as if that man is haunting me!' Both waking and asleep.

Sleep, despite her exhausted state, had been very hard to come by the previous night, thoughts of Jude Marshall, of the way he had kissed her, preventing her from drifting into a relaxed state.

What on earth had prompted him to kiss her at all? Oh, she knew that he was angry with her, a frustrated anger, at her total indomitableness. But she wouldn't have thought that was reason enough for him to have kissed her…?

David shrugged. 'He is rather—forceful.'

That was one way of describing him! All that May really knew at this moment was that her evening was completely ruined, the very fact that Jude was eating in the same room as her enough to put her off her food. Or to relax enough to enjoy David's company.

She sighed. 'He's a nuisance,' she acknowledged heavily.

David gave her a searching glance. 'Would you rather we ate somewhere else?'

She gave him an incredulous look. 'We can't do that!'

'Of course we can,' he assured her mildly.

May shook her head dazedly. 'But—but—we've ordered our food, and—and everything!' Even now she could see the waiter heading towards their table with their first course.

David shrugged. 'So we'll unorder it. The last thing I want, May,' he continued firmly as she would have protested again, 'is for you to feel under some sort of strain. The idea of this evening was for us to have a sociable dinner together, to relax and get to know each other a little better. Something we obviously aren't going to be able to do with Jude Marshall in the room.' He put his napkin down on the table and stood up to talk quietly to the waiter, the latter looking completely nonplussed as he returned to the kitchen still carrying the plates of food. 'I'll be back in two minutes,' David promised before striding over to the *maître d'*.

May watched him dazedly, hardly able to believe that David was willing to go to another restaurant just because he sensed how uncomfortable she was now that she knew Jude Marshall was dining here, too.

But as she saw Jude enter the dining-room at that moment, the beautiful woman who moved so gracefully

at his side, she knew that there was no way she could
have remained here now even if David had wanted to
do so.

The woman was tall and slender, her ebony dark hair
cut stylishly short, the glowing beauty of her face dom-
inated by luminous green eyes, her mouth a pouting invitation, the low-necked dress she wore revealing a
creamy expanse of shoulders and breasts, her legs long
and slender.

There was no doubting that, despite being in her for-
ties, the woman was absolutely stunning, and as she and
Jude walked to their table every pair of eyes in the room
followed their progress.

Except May's.

After that first glance she had got hastily to her feet,
not waiting for David to return but rushing quickly from
the room, not stopping until she reached the relative
sanctuary of the foyer, her breath coming in short gasps,
her pulse racing so fast she could feel the blood pulsing
through her veins.

What on earth was *she* doing here?

'Coward!' Jude murmured huskily.

May's shoulders had stiffened as she forked fresh hay
into the lambing pens, so he knew she was aware of his
presence behind her, but she made no effort to turn and
answer his accusation.

Because accusation it most certainly was.

Jude hadn't been able to believe it when, having seen
April seated opposite him at the dining table the previous
evening, he had turned to glance around the restaurant
in search of May and her own dining companion.

Only to find that she hadn't been there!

His mouth tightened. 'May, I said—'

'I heard what you said.' She turned sharply to face him, her features set in cool challenge as she looked at him questioningly.

He raised mocking dark brows. 'Well?'

'Well what?' she returned scathingly.

'Don't let's start that again!' He gave a disgusted shake of his head. 'Why did you leave the hotel so suddenly yesterday evening?'

'Did I?' she returned dismissively, obviously completely ignoring his frustration with the way she answered his questions with one of her own. Deliberately so? Probably, he acknowledged heavily.

Jude scowled. 'You know damn well you did.'

'We left the restaurant, Jude,' she corrected dryly. 'That doesn't mean we left the hotel,' she added pointedly.

Jude's scowl deepened as he easily understood her implication, his narrowed gaze searching on her almost defiant expression. If May were to be believed, then instead of eating she and David Melton had gone upstairs together to one of the hotel bedrooms...

'Besides,' she continued hardly, 'I'm surprised you even noticed our departure considering the identity of your own dining companion.' The last was added scornfully.

It wasn't easy, but Jude forced visions of May in David Melton's arms from his mind—for the present! He would get back to that subject in a moment.

His smile was mocking now. 'Ah, you recognised her,' he murmured with satisfaction.

May gave a derisive laugh. 'Along with everyone else in the room! But then, how could anyone not recognise the beautiful actress, April Robine?'

Jude wasn't sure he liked that scornful edge to May's

voice when she spoke of April. He had known the beautiful actress for several months now, had never found
her to be anything other than warm and charming, her
patience infinite with the fans who so often intruded
upon her privacy. Even yesterday evening as they had
been eating their meal, several people had come over to
their table to ask for her autograph, and none of them
had gone away disappointed, in April or the acquired
autograph.

'Your friend David certainly found her charming
when he came over to our table to say hello,' he bit out
caustically.

May was too startled by the statement to be able to
hide the emotion, her cheeks paling slightly, her eyes a
deeper green than usual. 'I don't know what you mean.'
She shook her head dismissively.

'I mean that April and your friend David apparently
know each other,' he bit out abruptly, having been surprised himself when David Melton had come over to
their table to be greeted so effusively by April. 'In fact,
from the warmth with which they kissed each other yesterday evening, you might say they know each other
very well!'

Jude frowned as May seemed to pale even more. Two
days ago May had assured him that she wasn't interested
in David Melton; in fact she had insisted, despite the
other man's obvious entreaties, that David Melton meant
nothing to her. And yet her reaction now to the other
man's acquaintance with the beautiful April seemed to
imply otherwise...

May moistened dry lips before visibly swallowing
hard. 'What does that have to do with me?'

He looked at her consideringly. 'Everything, I would
have thought—if your implication that you and David

spent the night together at the hotel is the correct one!' he rasped.

She drew in a sharp breath. 'For your information, I slept in my own bed last night!'

'Meaning that you and Melton only spent the evening in bed together at the hotel?' Jude scorned.

'Meaning that it's none of *your* damned business where I spent yesterday evening!' she returned forcefully.

He was going to shake her in a minute. Or kiss her again. Neither of which was a good idea.

He had learnt that only too well two days ago, could still feel the softness of her lips as they responded to his, the warmth of her curves as her body moulded against his. The very thought of David Melton enjoying those lips and her desirable softness was enough to make him forget everything else. And he didn't want to feel that way. Not over this woman. Or any other woman.

He drew in a deeply controlling breath. 'May, I actually came here to ask you to have dinner with me this evening.'

She straightened, eyeing him mockingly. 'Really?'

'Really,' he confirmed dryly.

May gave a shake of her head. 'Then you have a very strange way of going about it.'

Because he had been sidetracked by talk of her friendship with David Melton.

But it was time to forget about Melton, and April, and concentrate on what he really wanted from this woman.

'Okay,' he sighed frustratedly. 'Let's start again, shall we? May, will you have dinner with me this evening?'

'No,' she answered without hesitation, her gaze mocking. 'And just why is it that everyone seems to think I need to have dinner bought for me at the moment?' she added frowningly.

'Probably because you look as if a few good meals inside you wouldn't come amiss!' Jude's gaze moved deliberately down her obvious slenderness.

'Thanks,' she snapped. 'But the answer is still no!'

He scowled at her stubbornness. 'David Melton has booked you for this evening, too, hmm?'

'No—that's lunch,' she told him derisively, obviously enjoying his frustration.

Jude eyed her scathingly. 'So who's the lucky man tonight?'

'Do you mean to be insulting, Jude?' She quirked dark brows. 'Or does it just come naturally to you?'

His mouth twisted humourlessly. 'A little of both, I think.'

To his surprise she laughed softly, her eyes glowing deeply green, slight dimples beside the soft curve of her lips. God, she was beautiful, he acknowledged frowningly. Wearing no make-up that he could detect, her hair scraped back in an elastic band, wearing those awful clothes she worked in, and she was still beautiful. Too beautiful!

'Perhaps you wouldn't mind answering my question?' he rasped caustically.

She gave a slight shake of her head. 'I thought I already had. You asked me to have dinner with you, and I said no. Although I'm curious as to why you think you would ever have received any other sort of answer?' She looked at him searchingly.

'Because your mother brought you up to be polite?' he returned dryly—realising, too late, that her mother hadn't brought her up at all, that she had died while the three sisters were still babies.

May's eyes were now as hard as the jewels they resembled, her mouth unsmiling. 'Any manners I have certainly weren't taught me by my mother,' she snapped coldly. 'Although, again, I'm curious as to why you should think I would feel the need to be in the least polite to you?' she added with hard derision.

'Because I bought you dinner the other evening?' Jude shrugged, starting to find it decidedly warm in here in the thick Aran sweater and faded blue denims that he was wearing.

May gave him a quizzical look. 'In that case, shouldn't I be the one asking you out to dinner? To return the favour?'

'Not the most gracious invitation I've ever received— but I accept,' Jude told her, eyes gleaming with satisfaction.

She looked stunned by the deliberate trap he had set— and that she had unwittingly walked into. 'Now just a minute—'

'Too late, May,' he told her lightly. 'You asked, I accepted.'

'I did not—'

'You most certainly did,' he assured her mockingly, enjoying being the one to have completely disconcerted her this time.

'But I have an Amateur Dramatics meeting to go to this evening!' she protested frustratedly.

'Then I suggest you cancel it,' he dismissed unconcernedly. 'I'll leave you to book the restaurant, shall I? I prefer French cuisine if possible, but if not—'

'If you really expect me to give you dinner then you'll get May cuisine, you'll get it here—and like it!' she interrupted impatiently. 'Although—'

'Sounds great,' Jude accepted. 'About seven-thirty suit you?'

'Yes, but—'

'I'll bring the wine,' he continued happily, enjoying her dazed expression. 'Do you prefer red or white?'

'White. But—'

'Seven-thirty, then, May.' He nodded decisively.

May gave him a look of complete exasperation. 'You are the most arrogant, manipulative man it has ever been my misfortune to meet!' she finally burst out frustratedly.

He grinned. 'Takes one to know one,' he returned lightly.

Her eyes widened indignantly. 'I am not in the least arrogant or manipulative.'

'No?' he mocked. 'Well, perhaps I don't know you well enough yet to give a learned opinion,' he allowed softly.

Her eyes flashed angrily. 'And perhaps you never will know me well enough to give a learned opinion!'

He shrugged. 'We'll have to wait and see, won't we?' he dismissed. 'I'll leave you to get on with your work now, as you appear to have a date for lunch today, too,' he added hardly.

For someone who claimed she wasn't in the least interested in David Melton, May seemed to be seeing rather a lot of the other man. Not that it was any of his business, Jude reminded himself frowningly. It was probably just another example of what he considered to be the woman's contrariness!

'How kind of you,' May snapped back, obviously still angry at having been trapped into giving him dinner.

'I thought so.' Jude nodded, deciding this was probably a good time for him to leave.

After all, he would be seeing May later this evening, when they would hopefully have the time to talk more calmly about the offer he had made on this farm.

'With two good meals inside you today, you might actually start to put some weight on those bones, and so look a little less like a waif and stray,' he added hardly.

May was incredibly beautiful, breathtakingly so, but it was a beauty edged with an air of frailty, a certain look of delicacy that didn't suit the hard work she had to do living on a farm.

Although she didn't look too delicate at this moment, Jude acknowledged ruefully; instead she looked as if she would like to pick up the pitchfork she was still holding and stab him through the chest with it.

'For your information,' she bit out through gritted teeth, 'I am naturally slender! We all are,' she added defensively.

Jude gave her a considering look. 'I obviously can't speak for your sisters, May, never having met them,' he said dryly. 'But there's slender, and then there's gaunt—and I know which category you fit into at this moment!' he assured her dismissively.

'And when I want your opinion, Jude, I'll ask for it!' She turned her back on him and once again began forking the straw over in the empty pens.

Obviously that was the end of this particular conversation!

Jude gave a shrug, quite happy with what he had already achieved today. After all, she had called him Jude just now without any prompting from him. And with the promise of seeing May again this evening, he had every hope of achieving much more.

It was only once he was back in his car, driving down the rutted track that led up to the farm, that he realised

May, with this infuriating habit she had of answering his questions with one of her own, hadn't actually given him a sensible answer as to the reason she had left the restaurant so hastily the evening before…

CHAPTER FOUR

'FEELING better?' David prompted concernedly as the two of them sat in the bar of a pub not far from the farm.

'Much, thank you,' May answered huskily, guilty warmth entering her cheeks as she did so, not quite able to meet David's gaze, either.

She had been in an agitated state the previous evening when David had left the restaurant and joined her in the foyer of the hotel, able to feel it as her cheeks had first paled and then reddened, her eyes glittering brightly, as if with a fever, her movements agitated as she'd paced up and down waiting for him.

In the circumstances, it hadn't been too difficult for David to believe the lie that she hadn't been feeling well, that she would rather cancel dinner altogether and just go home.

And it hadn't been a complete lie, May had consoled herself; she had felt sick, and there was no way she could have eaten anything feeling the way that she had.

But she had agreed to have lunch with David today only as a means of escaping yesterday evening, still felt too nauseous to contemplate eating anything.

And Jude Marshall's visit to the farm this morning, a stark reminder of yesterday evening, had done little to alleviate that feeling!

She moistened dry lips. 'You said yesterday, David, that there is someone you would like me to meet...?'

'Why, yes.' He looked surprised at the change of subject.

May nodded. 'I believe I know who that someone is. And I have to tell you—'

'May, I simply thought over what we discussed in London a couple of weeks ago—' David sat forward in his seat, looking at her intently '—and I realised that you seemed to change after I had told you who the stars of the film were to be.' He gave her a sympathetic smile. 'I realise that working with big stars like Dan Howard and April Robine must have sounded a little overwhelming. But Dan is a great chap to work with, and as for April—'

'Jude mentioned that you went over to their table and spoke to her at the restaurant yesterday evening,' May put in stiltedly, if only to let him know how she had guessed who his 'someone' was.

David raised surprised brows. 'He did?'

'He did,' she confirmed, not about to get into a discussion about exactly when Jude had told her that; sufficient to say that May now knew exactly who David wanted her to meet while he was still in the area.

She also knew exactly why that meeting would never take place.

'I'm not in the least overwhelmed at the thought of working with April Robine, David,' she told him hardly, her jaw tightly clenched on her emotions. 'And I certainly have no desire to meet her,' she added harshly.

'But—'

'That is the end of the matter as far as I'm concerned,' May cut in decisively. 'You've been very kind.' Her voice softened slightly as she saw how hurt and confused David now looked. He was hurt and confused! 'But my answer is still no.'

David looked troubled. 'If you would just talk to April you would see—'

'No!' May cut in sharply, drawing in a deeply controlling breath as David looked stunned by her vehemence. 'I'm sorry—' she frowned '—but I really don't want this.'

There was no way she could tell him how much she didn't want it! But he at least had to believe how strongly she felt about all this. Without her actually having to spell the situation out in black and white...

Something she had no intention of doing. To anybody.

But David was perfectly correct in his assessment as to when her attitude to appearing in his film had changed. And it had nothing to do with Dan Howard!

David looked decidedly uncomfortable now. 'April really is a very charming woman.'

'I'm sure she is,' May bit out evenly.

'May—'

'David, I do apologize for being late,' interrupted a huskily breathless voice. 'We left in good time, but we had a little difficulty in finding the place.' The woman gave a ruefully dismissive laugh.

May had frozen into immobility at the first sound of that voice, couldn't breathe, couldn't move, certainly couldn't turn and look at the woman who had just joined them.

But she knew who it was, that huskily attractive voice unmistakable.

April Robine...

May had no doubts that David had set her up, had deliberately arranged for the actress to meet them here—in fact, the other woman's words confirmed that he had. No wonder David had looked so stricken seconds ago at May's vehement refusal to meet the famous actress.

May shot David an accusing glare as he looked at her concernedly before standing up to greet the other woman, every muscle in May's body tensed, all the air seeming to have been knocked out of her lungs as she shook badly.

This couldn't be happening!

It just couldn't be happening!

Her worst nightmare—but it was all too real!

May had thought, with her refusal of the part in David's film, that she had avoided this ever happening, that she could put it all from her mind once again. And, instead, she now found herself confronted with a woman she had no desire to meet—ever!

'May,' Jude Marshall greeted mockingly.

Now she did move, turning sharply in her seat to see Jude standing next to April Robine, his expression one of taunting challenge. Answering the 'we' in April Robine's initial statement...

But at least while May was looking at Jude she didn't have to look at the actress who stood at his side.

She was nevertheless completely aware of the other woman, could hear her talking softly to David, could smell the perfume she wore. A perfume that made May's head spin!

'Are you okay, May?' The mockery left Jude's face as he looked down at her concernedly.

'Of course I'm okay,' she replied brittlely as she stood up, willing the dizziness to dissipate; she was not going to faint. She was not! 'I didn't expect to see you here,' she added with husky rebuke.

He could so easily have told her earlier that he knew she wasn't lunching alone with David, that he and April Robine were to join them—giving May the opportunity not to appear!

But, then, maybe Jude had realised that? If not the actual reason for it...

'I didn't want to ruin the surprise for you,' Jude came back mockingly.

May gave a shaky sigh. 'These sort of surprises I can well do without.'

The humour left Jude's eyes as he looked down at her searchingly. 'You really don't look well, you know,' he finally murmured.

Her head went back challengingly. 'Maybe I'm just overwhelmed—' to use David's word! '—at finding myself in such exalted company!' she bit out scathingly.

This was awful. Terrible. Any second now she knew that David was going to introduce her to April Robine. What would the other woman's reaction be to such an introduction? Would she be as horrified as May was? Or something else? Whatever April Robine's reaction to meeting May, May had no doubts that the actress would hide it much better than she could.

Jude gave a slow shake of his head. 'I don't think too much overwhelms you, May,' he murmured frowningly.

He was right, it didn't. She had decided long ago that she was as good as anyone else, that she could do anything she chose to do, that nothing and no one had the power to unnerve her.

With the exception of April Robine...

'May—' David turned to lightly clasp her arm, drawing her to his side '—I would like to introduce you to April Robine. April, this is May Calendar,' he introduced happily.

May looked the other woman full in the face for the first time, the actress's beauty indisputable, her hair a short black cap surrounding flawless features, very slender in a deep green cashmere sweater and fitted black trousers, looking nowhere near middle-aged, which May knew the other woman to be.

There was also no hint of recognition in the other woman's eyes as she calmly returned May's gaze.

Jude watched May concernedly as the introductions were made, her cheeks unnaturally pale, green eyes appearing huge against that paleness. He was convinced, no matter what she might claim to the contrary, that something was seriously wrong with her.

'Miss Robine,' she was greeting now, the words forced through her clenched jaw.

'Oh, please do call me April,' the beautiful actress requested with her usual warmth. 'And may I call you May?'

Jude was still watching May, saw the nerve pulsing in her throat as she swallowed convulsively. What on earth—?

'I would rather you called me Miss Calendar,' she answered the other woman abruptly. 'As I would rather call you Miss Robine,' she added dismissively.

What on earth was wrong with her? Jude finished his earlier thought incredulously in the tense silence that followed May's rude statement.

May had been annoyed with him when they'd first met, had plenty of reason to dislike him, but even so she had never spoken to him in this coldly dismissive voice. From the little he had come to know of her the last few days, he doubted she had ever spoken to anyone quite like this before.

Maybe he should have prewarned her about this meeting, after all; it would certainly have given her time to get used to the idea.

She was probably just nervous, he allowed. After all,

April had been an internationally acclaimed actress since she'd taken Hollywood by storm almost twenty years ago, was recognised wherever she went, was highly respected by her fellow actors and the public alike. This must be a little like meeting an icon, someone you had thought untouchable as well as unreachable.

Yes, that had to be it. As soon as May realised how warm and friendly April was, she would start to relax. She might even start to enjoy herself...

'That's a ridiculous idea, May,' he dismissed lightly as he moved to hold back a chair for April to sit down. 'If we're all going to have lunch together—'

'Oh, but we aren't,' May answered him tautly, her bag clutched between tightly clenched fingers now. 'I'm afraid I've just remembered something else I have to do, so if you'll all excuse me—'

'No, we won't excuse you!' Jude was the one to answer sharply, David Melton looking on in mute shock, April appearing a little less than her normally composed self, too.

As well she might!

It was perfectly natural for May to feel nervous about meeting April; it wasn't acceptable for her to continue to be rude about it!

Jude drew in a deeply controlling breath, aware that the four of them were attracting a certain amount of attention now from the other people in this lounge bar— and not all of it was because they had recognised April. It must be obvious to even the casual observer that there was a definite air of tension between the four of them.

'Look, let's just all sit down and have a drink together,' Jude suggested lightly. 'We can discuss then whether or not we intend eating lunch, hmm?' He looked at May encouragingly.

She returned his gaze unblinkingly, her expression completely unreadable, her eyes cold. 'As I've already told you, I have something else I need to do.' Her cold mask slipped slightly as she turned to look at David Melton. 'I'm really sorry about this, David.' She spoke huskily. 'But I—you should have warned me!' She turned on her heel and almost ran across the room.

As if the devil himself were at her heels.

'May—'

'Leave her, Jude,' April said, reaching up to put a restraining hand on his arm as he would have turned to follow May from the room.

'Like hell I will!' he rasped, easily moving away, one glance at the hurt so visible in April's beautiful eyes enough to propel him into action.

Jude strode purposefully from the room, almost bumping into May as he found her standing just outside, closing the door behind him as he swung her round to face him. 'What the hell do you—?' He broke off his angry tirade, frowning darkly as he saw the tears coursing down her cheeks. 'May…?' He blinked his utter confusion with this whole situation.

'Leave me alone!' she choked, pulling away from him. 'All of you, just leave me alone!' She glared up at him. 'Go back inside to your—your friend!' she added accusingly, frantically searching through her handbag now for her car keys.

Jude looked down at her frustratedly, totally thrown by the tears still falling down her cheeks. He had followed her intending to give her a good shaking, to demand an explanation for her rude behaviour, but he could see by her tears that there was more going on here than he had at first realised.

'Is it because of what I said to you earlier about David

Melton's obvious pleasure at seeing April when he came over to our table at the restaurant yesterday evening?' he probed frowningly. 'Do you think he's involved with April? Is that what's upsetting you?'

'David...?' May stared up at him uncomprehendingly. 'David?' she repeated impatiently. 'I don't know what you're talking about, Jude.' She shook her head dismissively, having at last found her car keys.

'I'm talking about the fact that you were damned rude in there just now.' He nodded in the direction of the bar.

'Was I rude to you?' May challenged hardly, eyes overbright.

'No, of course—'

'Was I rude to David?' she snapped.

'I wouldn't give a damn if you were rude to him—'

'Then it must have been April Robine I was rude to,' May bit out scornfully.

'You know very well that it was.' Jude was fast losing any patience he might still have had with her.

May eyed him mockingly. 'And that upsets you?'

'Of course it—' He broke off, taking several deeply controlling breaths. He never raised his voice in anger, never became angry if at all possible; anger had a habit of making logical thought impossible, behaviour irrational, and those were two things he didn't allow. 'May, for goodness' sake tell me what's wrong with you?' he prompted evenly.

'Wrong with me?' she repeated tauntingly. 'Why, nothing is *wrong with me*, Jude. I've already told you, I simply have something else I have to do.'

'So important that you have to go and do it right now? So urgent that you can't even sit down and have lunch with us first?' he said disbelievingly.

'Yes,' she answered flatly.

His mouth tightened. 'And the tears? I suppose they're for nothing, too?'

Her eyes flashed angrily. 'Let's leave my tears out of it—'

'No—let's not,' Jude rasped harshly, grasping her shoulders. 'I want to know what's going on, May—and you're going to tell me,' he assured her grimly.

'No-I-am-not!' she bit out between gritted teeth, at the same time trying to pull away from him.

Jude had no idea what all this was about, couldn't even begin to understand what was making her behave in this strange way. And he didn't like feeling in the dark in this way!

He stared down at her impotently, anger fighting with his sheer frustration over the situation. There was only one way he had found to subdue this woman—

'Let me go, Jude!' May ordered coldly, as if she had already guessed what his intention was.

'No.' He shook his head uncompromisingly. 'I—ouch!' He gave an involuntary cry of pain as May turned her head and bit the side of his hand, releasing her abruptly to look disbelievingly at the teethmarks clearly visible on his skin. 'What the hell did you do that for?' He looked at her dumbfoundedly.

She gave an unconcerned shrug. 'I asked you to release me, you refused—'

'And that was reason enough to bite me?' He scowled darkly.

May gave a humourless smile. 'It's okay, Jude, I'm not rabid or anything—'

'Going on the evidence of the last few minutes, I wouldn't be too sure about that!' he muttered disgustedly.

Her mouth tightened, her expression bleak. 'If you

want answers to your questions, Jude, then I suggest you go back in there and ask them of April Robine—although I can't guarantee they will be truthful ones,' she added scornfully.

Jude became suddenly still. April was the problem here, not David Melton, after all...?

Jude hated it when he didn't know what was going on. Hated it even more knowing May had no intention of enlightening him...

'Maybe I'll do that,' he said slowly.

'Fine,' May snapped hardly. 'Would you tell David—?'

'I'm not telling David anything!' Jude cut in scathingly. 'I'm not your messenger-boy, May; if you have something to say to David Melton, then go back in and tell him yourself!'

She drew in a sharp breath, glancing at the pub door, eyes so dark a green now they looked almost as black as the pupil. 'I'll pass, thank you,' she murmured huskily, grimacing slightly. 'I've already kept you from your lunch long enough,' she added dismissively.

Jude continued to stare at her frustratedly for several long seconds before giving a rueful shake of his head. 'I doubt any of us will feel like eating after what just happened!'

She gave a cool inclination of her head. 'That's your prerogative.'

'No, May—that's the situation you have created,' he rebuked harshly.

'I didn't create it—*she* did!' she returned forcefully, giving an impatient shake of her head as she seemed to realise she had said too much. 'I really do have to go, Jude,' she said shakily. 'I—you—you just don't understand!' she cried shakily.

'Then enlighten me!' he pressured frustratedly.

'I—I can't!' She shook her head firmly. 'I'm sorry, Jude. Really sorry,' she choked intensely before turning and hurrying over to unlock her car.

Jude made no move to re-enter the pub, stood in the porchway watching as May drove away, more confused by what had just happened than he would like to admit.

May had spoken just now as if she and April had already met before today, that it was some sort of past conflict between the two women that had caused her behaviour just now. And yet April's own behaviour hadn't implied any such conflict on her part, and she had made no mention on the way here of already being acquainted with May.

But perhaps April hadn't known it was May that David Melton had intended introducing her to today?

No, that didn't make any sense, either, because April had been as graciously charming as always even after the introductions had been made. So maybe the resentment was all on May's side, and for something so obscure April didn't even have knowledge of it?

Jude gave a puzzled shake of his head. It was one explanation for May's behaviour just now, but surely the two women must have met at some time for this situation to have developed, even if April seemed to have forgotten the incident?

Which gave rise to yet another puzzling question: how on earth could two such disparate women as May Calendar and April Robine have possibly met before? And when?

Although English, April had lived in America for almost twenty years, most of her work based there, too.

And as far as Jude was aware, May had rarely been away from her beloved farm, even for holidays.

Ask April for the answers he wanted to his questions, May had told him—but with a seeming certainty that those answers wouldn't be truthful ones...

CHAPTER FIVE

'MAY...'

May swayed slightly in the action of climbing down from the cab of the tractor she had just driven back into the yard.

Having hurried home several hours earlier from that luncheon appointment she had believed was with David alone, she had filled the rest of the afternoon and early evening with the regular but necessary jobs about the farm.

She had been expecting this visit, of course, but, even so, now that it had happened she still felt the shock of recognition moving chillingly down the length of her spine.

'May, I think the two of us need to talk—don't you?' April Robine prompted huskily.

May deliberately kept her back turned to the other woman, fighting to control the array of emotions she knew must be moving swiftly across her expressive face.

There had been no car visible in the yard a few moments ago to tell her of the other woman's presence here, no pre-warning of this confrontation. The only positive thing about it that May could see was that she was alone here on the farm, that neither of her sisters were here to witness this.

'May?'

She stiffened her spine, turning slowly to face the other woman as she continued to step down onto the cobbled yard, at the same time registering the red car parked beside the garage, and so not visible to anyone entering from the lane. As May had done...

She looked up resentfully at the other woman. 'You knew I didn't want you to come here.' It was at once a statement and an accusation.

The actress looked less controlled than she had at lunchtime today, lines of strain beside her eyes, her face pale beneath her impeccable make-up, still dressed in the cashmere sweater and fitted black trousers she had worn earlier.

'In fact,' May continued derisively, 'I'm surprised you could still find your way here!'

April Robine flinched as May's deliberate taunt obviously hit home. 'I remember everything about this place, May—'

'Really?' she cut in scathingly. 'Then you'll remember the way out again, won't you?' She turned away, moving to unfasten the trailer from the back of the tractor, her hands shaking as much with rage as shock.

How dared this woman come here? How dared she!

No—she wouldn't cry. Wouldn't give this woman the satisfaction of knowing how much her mere presence here, of all places, hurt and upset her.

'Still here?' she taunted as she turned to find the actress standing as if frozen.

April Robine looked at her searchingly, her face having lost all colour now. 'I was sorry to hear about your father last year—'

'Were you?' May cut in hardly, her hands clenching at her sides. 'Were you really?' she repeated scornfully.

April's eyes flashed angrily at May's obvious scepticism. 'Yes, I was really,' she snapped. 'I—he was—James and I may have had our differences, but I never wished him any harm—'

'Oh, please,' May muttered disgustedly. 'Spare me the insincere platitudes!'

'They aren't insincere,' the actress sighed. 'Far from it. May, you were very young, you can have no idea—'

'No idea of what?' May glared at the other woman. 'Of my father's unhappiness because his wife had left him?' She gave a disbelieving shake of her head. 'I may have been ''very young'', as you put it, but I wasn't too young to see that my father lost the will to live himself after you left, that it was only because of his three children that he managed to carry on at all!' Her face was flushed, her eyes feverish, her breasts quickly rising and falling beneath her thick black sweater as she breathed agitatedly.

'They were my three children, too!' April cried emotionally, her hands raised appealingly.

May became very still, all anger leaving her as that chill once more settled down her spine.

January. March. May. Yes, they had been this woman's three children. And she had left them as well as their father, had walked out on all of them to follow a star, to become a star herself.

And two weeks ago David Melton had ironically offered May the film role of Stella, with April Robine playing the title role of Stella's mother!

May had been so excited when David, a well-established film director both in England and America, had picked her out of a local pantomime as a possible actress in the film he was shooting this summer, claiming that she was perfect for the part of Stella, the heroine's daughter. But all of that excitement had died the moment David had told her who was to play the part of her mother.

David had claimed May was perfect for the part.

Of course May was perfect for the part!

David couldn't know how perfect...

Because April Robine really *was* her mother!

For years she had denied that fact, by tacit agreement with her father had brought January and March up with the impression that their mother had died while they were still very young. Only to have the woman brought vividly back to life in this intrusive way!

May looked coldly at the other woman. 'Our mother is dead,' she stated flatly.

April gasped, her face paling even more. 'Is that what January and March think, too?' she choked disbelievingly.

'It's what we all think,' May assured her hardly. 'Only I know that my mother was a beautiful, selfish woman, who cared more about fame and fortune than she did for her husband and three young daughters. She died for all of us the moment she made that choice,' she added coldly.

April swallowed hard, her beautiful face pale and haggard as she looked every inch her forty-six years. 'I knew James hated me, but I never thought—'

'He didn't hate you,' May cut in incredulously. 'He loved you. Only you. Until the day he died,' she concluded emotionally, knowing it was the truth, that their father had never looked at another woman in the years after April had left him, that he had continued to love his ex-wife despite what she had done.

April closed her eyes briefly, swaying slightly. 'There didn't have to be a choice,' she breathed shakily. 'Your father—'

'I absolutely refuse to discuss my father with you!' May cut in forcefully, glaring at the other woman. 'I lived with him for over twenty years after you left, I saw what your leaving did to him—so don't presume to come here all these years later and tell me anything about him!' She breathed agitatedly.

The other woman swallowed hard. 'We have to talk, May—'

'Why do we?' she challenged. 'I have nothing to say to you. And, after all these years, I can't believe you have anything to say to me, either!' she added scathingly.

The beautiful face softened with emotion. 'Do you have any idea how I felt when David told me that the young woman he had picked out to play opposite me in his next film was called May Calendar?'

May grimaced scornfully. 'I can imagine!'

'No, you can't,' April contradicted softly.

'If it was anything like the way I felt when I learnt you were the star of the film, then, yes, I can!' May insisted hardly.

She had been so shocked, so stunned by the knowledge, that she had hurried home on the next train back to Yorkshire from her screen test in London, informing her sisters that she had turned down David's offer, and that she didn't wish to discuss the subject any further, knowing only too well David kept insisting why she was perfect to play opposite April Robine in the role of her daughter.

The actress shook her head. 'Somehow I don't think so,' she murmured softly. 'Tell me about January and March. Are they—?'

'They are none of your business!' May assured her hardly, wondering when this nightmare was going to be over.

April's mouth firmed determinedly. 'Jude tells me that they are engaged to marry two of his closest friends—'

'You've told Jude that we're your daughters?' May gasped disbelievingly.

The other woman raised derisive brows. 'What do you think?'

May gave a disgusted snort. 'I think you wouldn't want Jude, of all people, to know you have three daughters aged in their mid to late twenties!'

After all, Jude was around ten years younger than the woman he was obviously intimately involved with—to know that she had three such grown-up daughters, not that much younger than himself, would be a bit of a dampener on the relationship, May would have thought!

April frowned darkly. 'That isn't the reason I haven't told him. May, I don't know what impression you've formed of my being with Jude earlier today, but I can assure you—'

'I don't need or want your assurances, Miss Robine— on anything!' May cut in coldly. 'And neither do January and March—'

'You can't speak for them,' the other woman protested.

'In this case, yes, I can,' May said with certainty. 'They grew up all these years without a mother, they certainly don't need one now that they are about to marry the men they love!'

'Especially one like me, is that it?' April finished flatly.

'That's it.' May nodded firmly, wishing the other woman would just leave, the strain of these last few minutes beginning to tell. She turned away, not sure how much longer she was going to last before she broke down in tears.

This was her mother, for goodness' sake, the mother she had adored for the first five years of her life, the woman she had had to learn to live without after April had walked out on her husband and children to pursue her acting career. Just the smell of April's remembered perfume earlier today had been enough to make her head spin.

'I've given David my answer concerning the film role; I don't think we have anything more to say to each other?' Her expression was deliberately challenging.

'David tells me you're a very good actress,' April prompted huskily.

She shrugged. 'He seems to think so.'

April nodded. 'And exactly where do you think that acting talent came from?'

May's eyes flashed deeply green. 'The same place that January's singing talent and March's artistic one came from, I expect!' she snapped, knowing that none of them had inherited those talents from their staid, unimaginative father.

'January sings and March paints?' April murmured incredulously.

'Yes—but I'm sure we would all willingly give up those talents not to have you as our mother!' May came back insultingly.

April paled even more. 'Are you giving up your chance of stardom because I happen to be in the film, too?' The other woman gave a pained frown.

May gave her a scathing glance. 'Some of us do have our priorities in the proper order!'

April flinched at the deliberate taunt, her chin rising challengingly as she looked at May with narrowed eyes. 'You—' She broke off as both of them became aware of the sound of an approaching vehicle. 'Are you expecting anyone?' April prompted frowningly.

Jude!

It had to be him, a brief glance at her wrist-watch having told May that it was seven-thirty, the time Jude had said this morning that he would arrive for dinner this evening, with a bottle of white wine.

After their conversation at lunchtime she hadn't thought for a moment that Jude would keep their dinner engagement for this evening, but the timing was too much of a coincidence for it not to be him.

Damn!

What was she going to say about April Robine being here? More to the point, what was April Robine going to say about her own presence here?

Jude's foot almost slipped off the accelerator as he drove into the farmyard to see May and April standing there obviously deep in conversation.

What on earth was April doing here? A muddy farmyard was positively the last place he would ever have expected to find the beautifully elegant actress, he acknowledged with amusement, the contrast between the two women even more extreme now that May was back in her working clothes, that woollen cap once again pulled down over her hair.

Remembering May's deliberate rudeness to the other woman earlier today, her absolute adamance that she had nothing to say to April, he was more than a little puzzled to find the two of them here together this evening...

He parked his car beside April's red one, getting out to slowly walk over to join them. 'Ladies,' he greeted lightly, giving them both a quizzical look.

'Jude!' April was the one to greet lightly. 'I had no idea you were coming here this evening,' she added teasingly.

He gave a slight inclination of his head, still completely in the dark as to exactly what was going on between these two women, and as such reluctant to commit himself either way. 'I had no idea you were coming here, either,' he returned noncommittally.

May gave a disgusted snort. 'Have you ever noticed how Jude answers a question with a question?' she derided.

April gave him a considering look, head tilted enchantingly to one side. 'Now that you mention it—'

'I actually answered a statement with a statement this time,' Jude defended curtly, having the strange feeling, despite these two women's obvious differences, that they were somehow in league at this particular moment.

'Same difference,' May dismissed mockingly. 'The end result, of your giving out very little information, is still the same,' she expanded as he raised questioning brows.

'Perhaps,' he allowed guardedly.

May gave April a knowing look. 'See what I mean!' she derided.

April smiled warmly. 'I do.'

Jude raised dark brows. 'Are you invited for dinner, too, April?'

'No!'

'I don't—'

Both women began talking at once, May emphatically in the negative, April a little more ambiguous.

'I don't think I'm invited,' April finished ruefully.

'Pity,' Jude murmured after a brief glance at May's stubbornly set expression.

It would have been interesting watching the interplay between these two such different women—he might even have learnt some of the reason for the antipathy between them, on May's part, at least. April, he realised, was more unsettled than angry.

'I'll leave you two to your dinner, then,' April dismissed lightly, seeming to take some effort to gather her usual equilibrium, her smile bright and meaningless, certainly not accompanied by the usual warmth of her eyes.

Jude eyed May mockingly. 'I'm not sure May has remembered that she invited me, either!' he drawled derisively, the fact that she was obviously dressed for working on the farm not looking too promising.

No doubt after their fraught conversation at lunchtime May had decided that he wouldn't be coming for dinner this evening after all; it afforded him a certain amount of satisfaction to know that he had disconcerted her by arriving, after all. But not too much—he still had no idea what the tension was between May and April.

'I remembered the invitation,' May assured him dryly. 'The chicken casserole has been in the oven for several hours.'

It might have been, but Jude still doubted that May had ever thought he would be joining her this evening to eat it!

'Enough for three?' he prompted pointedly.

May's expression darkened. 'I—'

'I'm sorry, but I already have a dinner engagement for this evening,' April cut in smoothly. 'In fact—' she glanced at her gold wrist-watch '—I had better be going, or I shall be late.' She turned to May. 'I hope I shall see you again before I leave,' she said huskily.

'How long are you staying in the area?' May looked at her coldly.

April shrugged narrow shoulders. 'I'm not sure yet...'

May nodded abruptly. 'Well, in case I don't see you again, have a safe journey home,'

In other words, Jude easily interpreted, however long you happen to be staying in the area, don't come back here to see me!

This really was a very strange situation, an even stranger conversation—one that Jude, for one, found completely puzzling.

'Thank you,' April accepted heavily, her smile even more strained as she turned to Jude. 'I'll probably see you later.'

He nodded abruptly. 'You can count on it.'

She gave a rueful smile. 'I thought I might! I-it really was lovely to meet you, May,' she added huskily.

A sentiment that May, Jude noted frowningly, had no intention of echoing. In fact, she looked so cold and unapproachable she might have been carved from ice.

What was this?

What possible reason could May have for feeling so antagonistic towards April? An antagonism, he now realised, despite April's apparent calm at lunchtime, that her presence here this evening meant she was equally aware of.

As he watched April walk over to her car, her face deathly pale as she drove out of the farmyard, Jude vowed that he would get an answer to those questions, either from May or April, he didn't really care which.

CHAPTER SIX

MAY eyed Jude surreptitiously as the red car turned out of the farmyard, taking April Robine with it, knowing that Jude must be completely confused at finding the actress here when he arrived after the way the meeting had gone between the two women at lunchtime, that he must be completely puzzled about the whole situation.

Well, she for one had no intention of enlightening him. And, after her brief conversation with April Robine as Jude had arrived, she knew that the other woman wasn't about to do so, either.

April Robine...

Strange that was the only way that May could think of the other woman, but also knowing the reason for that was probably that she refused to recognise her as the mother who had deserted her when she was only a child of five.

What sort of woman did that? Walked out, not only on her husband, but on her three young daughters, aged only five, four, and three? Not one that May wanted to know, or be associated with, that was for sure!

She drew in a harsh breath, her gaze deliberately non-committal as she looked at Jude. 'If you would like to go into the kitchen and get warm, I'll join you in a few minutes,' she dismissed, knowing a few minutes wouldn't be near long enough to her to compose herself after speaking to April Robine, but at the same time recognising that was all the time she had.

'I'm not cold,' Jude dismissed evenly, despite the icy

wind whistling through the farmyard. 'In fact, I think the
air in the kitchen might be even more chilly than it is
out here!' he added pointedly.

'Really? The Aga keeps it very warm in there, I can
assure you.' May was deliberately obtuse.

'I wasn't referring to the heating system, and you
know it!' Jude rasped, gaze narrowed to silver slits as
he looked down at her probingly.

'Do I?' She shrugged, turning away. 'I just have to
check on the— What do you think you're doing?' She
gasped as Jude grasped her arm and swung her roughly
back to face him.

'Are you going to tell me what's going on, or do I
have to find out for myself?' he prompted harshly.

May stared up at him frowningly. This man was probably her mother's lover, had probably been so for some
time; if anyone owed him any explanations it certainly
wasn't her!

Her mouth firmed determinedly. 'Why don't you ask
April Robine?' she snapped. 'Although the two of you
seem to have a very—relaxed relationship, considering
you're here having dinner with me and she's off to have
dinner with someone else!' she added insultingly.

Jude's gaze narrowed even more. 'And what's that
supposed to mean?'

May shrugged. 'Whatever you want it to mean.' She
sighed, suddenly realising she was too weary to get involved in another situation of conflict. 'It's been a long
day already, Jude, and I'm tired and I'm hungry, so do
you think we could postpone this—whatever this is—
until after we've eaten?'

He looked down at her for several tension-filled
minutes, before slowly releasing her arm, a mocking
smile curving his lips now. 'You weren't expecting me

to turn up for dinner this evening as arranged, were you?' he murmured with amusement.

'In all honesty? No,' she confirmed dryly. 'But then, you're a man that likes to do the unexpected, aren't you?' She shrugged. 'Probably as another means of putting people off their guard,' she guessed shrewdly, knowing by the way his mouth tightened that she was right in her assessment. Well, he needn't have bothered on her account this evening—she had already been well and truly 'put off her guard' before he'd even arrived!

'And you're a woman who likes to analyse too much,' he dismissed. 'I'll go and get the wine from the car.'

May watched him as he strode away, his movements fluid, the icy wind stirring the darkness of his hair, his masculine vitality unmistakable.

What was his relationship to April Robine? Lover? Friend? What? May had no idea, but until she did it would be foolish of her to allow her own attraction to him to go any further than it already had.

Which wasn't all that easy to do when he deliberately set himself out to be charming as they ate their meal together later, telling her several amusing stories about Max, Will and himself when they were at school together, the earlier tension seemingly forgotten. And yet May knew that it wasn't. Not really. By either of them...

'Do you have any other family beside your parents, Jude?' she prompted curiously as they lingered over coffee and an orange-based liqueur she had found at the back of the cupboard, given to them a couple of years ago as a Christmas present and never opened.

He grimaced. 'Siblings, that sort of thing, do you mean?'

'That sort of thing,' she confirmed dryly; since the death of her father the previous year, her sisters were the two most important people in her life, and not to be so easily dismissed.

'I'm an only child, I'm afraid.' Jude shrugged. 'Probably just as well, considering the amount of toing and froing I had to do between America and England during my childhood.' He grimaced. 'I don't think we ever lived in the same house for more than a couple of years.'

Which probably also accounted for his seeming lack of roots now. It would also explain his complete lack of understanding where her attachment to this family farm was concerned...

'I know where you're going with this, May.' He sat back, smiling.

She sighed. 'Do you?'

'I think so.' He nodded. 'But it doesn't change the fact that this farm is too much for you to manage alone.'

She bristled resentfully, still not completely over April Robine's visit here earlier. 'No doubt April Robine echoes your sentiments,' she snapped, having no doubts the other woman was completely mystified concerning May's stubbornness about selling this farm to Jude; twenty-two years ago she hadn't been able to get away fast enough!

'April?' Jude echoed frowningly. 'What on earth does she have to do with any of this?'

May blinked, realising—too late—that she had allowed her personal resentment towards the other woman to show once again. And in a way Jude couldn't possibly understand. 'Well—'

'I don't discuss my business dealings with April, if that's what you're implying, May,' he assured her hardly.

Her eyes widened. 'Why don't you?'

'Because I— May, exactly what sort of relationship is it you think I have with April?' he prompted slowly.

She shrugged. 'The two of you obviously arrived here together, are staying at the hotel together—'

'We arrived together because I was coming over on business anyway, and it turned out April had some business of her own to take care of in the area, too,' he said with a pointed look in May's direction. 'And although we're both staying at the same hotel—'

'You really don't owe me any explanations, Jude,' May cut in, standing up abruptly, deciding she really didn't want to know what this man's relationship was to her mother.

Because in spite of everything, his increasingly pressurised efforts to buy the farm by his sheer presence every time she turned around, his friendship with April, she was attracted to him herself.

Jude turned to look at her. 'Don't I, May?' he said softly, standing up himself now.

May looked across at him with widely apprehensive eyes. Too much had already happened today; she simply couldn't cope if Jude were to kiss her again.

Which, it seemed, he had every intention of doing!

She fitted so well against him as he took her in his arms, the curves of her body fitting perfectly into his, her mouth responding to the touch of his like a flower to the sun.

It was all so simple when Jude held her like this, kissed her like this; nothing else mattered. It was only—

She couldn't think any more, could only feel, her arms moving up about his neck as the kissed deepened, became more demanding, Jude's hands moving restlessly up and down her spine, quivers of warmth moving through her wherever he touched.

'You're so beautiful, May,' Jude breathed huskily as his lips travelled the length of her creamy throat, his tongue seeking the hollows he found there, teeth gently biting her earlobe.

May shivered with desire, feeling engulfed by a warmth she had never known before, knowing that she wanted this man, wanted him as she had never wanted any other, that she longed for the hard nakedness of him against her own heated flesh.

How could she feel any other way with Jude kissing her like this, touching her like this, one of his hands moving to cup her breast now, the silk of the blouse she had changed into earlier no barrier to his caress as his thumb moved rhythmically against her hardened nipple?

He drew in a deeply controlling breath, his hands now moving up to frame the warmth of her face, his forehead resting on hers as he looked into her eyes. 'I want to make love with you, May,' he groaned huskily. 'And I think you want to make love with me, too,' he added softly.

She drew in a quivering breath, knowing it was what she wanted, too, wanted more than she had ever wanted anything in her life before, felt as if she might wilt and die if Jude didn't make love to her. Now!

Which was ridiculous when they were in the kitchen, the only place for them to make love on the coldness of the flagstones beneath their feet...

'But I don't want any regrets, May,' Jude continued gently, his thumbs lightly caressing her creamy cheeks, his silver gaze easily holding hers.

May couldn't break that gaze, trapped in the emotions

coursing through her, feeling on fire with need of him. She wanted him—how she wanted him.

'Will it help if I assure you that there is nothing between April and myself?' he prompted at her continued silence.

May stiffened as if he had struck her, suddenly cold as ice in Jude's arms, her eyes wide with shock.

April!

April Robine!

The woman who had once been her mother.

Jude inwardly cursed himself as he saw the change come over May at the mere mention of the other woman, the way her eyes had widened, lost their dreamy arousal to focus sharply, her body suddenly stiff as a board even as she began to push him away from her.

She turned away. 'I think you had better go,' she choked, her face buried in her hands.

'May—'

'No, Jude!' She moved sharply away from his reaching hands, turning fully to face him, green eyes dark with an emotion it was impossible to read. 'I invited you here for dinner, Jude, not to—'

'Don't be any more insulting than you need to be, May,' he cut in raspingly. 'I kissed you. You responded.' He gave an impatient shake of his head. 'Don't try and make it less—or more, than it was.' He looked at her with narrowed eyes.

She gathered herself together with effort, standing tall, straightening her shoulders determinedly. 'Yes, by all means, let's be adult about this, Jude,' she bit out. 'After all, that's what we both are, isn't it?' she dismissed with forced brightness.

He didn't want to be adult about this, wanted to grasp her by the shoulders and give her a thorough shaking.

Which would achieve precisely what? he prompted self-derisively.

Not a hell of a lot, he acknowledged, but it might make him feel a temporary respite from the sheer frustration he felt at this whole situation.

He wanted May, he admitted it. Wanted her pretty badly. But so many things stood between them, it seemed, not least his friendship with April.

Which was something he definitely didn't understand. And May had no intention of confiding in him…

He gave her a searching look. 'Why didn't you tell me that you're an actress, that the reason David Melton is being so persistent is because he wants you to take a part in one of his films?'

He saw May's eyes widen at the fact that he even knew that much about her. Well, damn it, he had certainly wanted some sort of explanation from David and April for what had happened at lunchtime. Besides, what was wrong with David Melton having told him that much, at least? It had certainly put his own mind at rest concerning the other man's intentions towards May.

He only wondered at May's complete determination that she would never appear in that film…

'Wanting and getting are two different things,' May answered him tautly. 'I'm sure David must also have told you that I've turned down his offer? Several times.'

His mouth twisted. Yes, the other man had been most emphatic concerning his interest in May. 'He told me.' He nodded. 'He was a little hazy as to why, though,' Jude added slowly.

'Was he?' May gave a humourless smile.

Jude looked at her searchingly. 'Is it because of your determination to hang onto this farm?'

Something flickered in those normally candid green eyes, something that was masked before he had time to even begin to analyse it—giving him the distinct impression that whatever May was about to say in answer to his question, it was far from the truth.

He also knew that, until this moment, the one thing May had given him had been honesty—no matter how insulting or rude it might have been!

'Yes, that's it,' she dismissed easily.

Too easily, too smoothly, Jude knew, his frustration with this situation deepening. 'I don't believe you,' he bit out hardly.

Her eyes widened mockingly. 'And is that supposed to bother me?' She gave a rueful shake of her head. 'Jude, I think you have an overinflated opinion of your own importance. Especially where I'm concerned!' Her eyes flashed warningly.

'May...!' he snapped impatiently, knowing she was back to being deliberately insulting.

Her brows rose tauntingly. 'Jude?'

His mouth thinned angrily. She was the most difficult woman it had ever been his misfortune to meet. Seconds ago she had been responsive and pliant in his arms, on the brink, it seemed to him, of the two of them making love together, and now she was back to being that mockingly defensive woman that just made him want to shake her until her teeth rattled.

Which action would get them about as far as her deliberate antagonism.

'May, you—' He broke off as she suddenly looked startled before moving quickly to the kitchen window. 'May, what is it?' He frowned his irritation.

'I'm not sure—oh, no...!' she groaned achingly, her face white as she turned from looking out of the window. 'I—it's—what have you done, Jude?' she groaned accusingly.

He looked startled. 'Me? But—'

'You knew I didn't want— How *could* you—? What am I going to do now?' she wailed emotionally.

'What the hell are you talking about?' Jude demanded impatiently even as he strode purposefully over to look out of the window, easily recognising at least two of the people getting out of the car that was now parked in the yard. And having recognised Max and Will, it wasn't too difficult to work out that the two beautiful dark-haired women with them, their likeness to May apart, had to be their fiancées, January and March.

Or to know, by one glance down at the anxiety on May's face, that her two sisters were the last people she wanted to see right now.

And from the accusing way she had looked at him just now, the way she had spoken, she obviously believed he had something to do with her sisters arriving back here so unexpectedly.

CHAPTER SEVEN

'How *could* you?' May demanded again, tears of frustration brimming in her eyes. 'You *knew* I didn't want them back here—'

'May, whatever you may think of me,' Jude cut in forcefully, 'I did not tell anyone that you were managing here alone, least of all your sisters, or Max and Will.'

She stared at him for several long seconds, not sure whether she believed him or not, but knowing that she didn't have time at this moment to debate the subject.

She turned agitatedly. 'You have to go,' she told Jude forcefully, clasping her hands together so tightly that the knuckles turned white. 'No—you have to stay,' she amended frantically, moving agitatedly about the room now as she tried to decide what she should do for the best, all the time her brain racing.

January and March were the last people she wanted back here, now of all times, May all too conscious of the fact that April Robine was only miles away. And that January and March had no idea, despite the fact that the woman was an internationally acclaimed actress, that she was also their mother.

While they were all growing up it had never occurred to May that either of her sisters need ever know that their mother hadn't really died twenty-two years ago but had deserted them. Even once May had realised that the actress who had become April Robine was their mother, it hadn't seemed necessary to tell her sisters the truth; after all, what were the chances of any of them ever meeting the famous actress, by accident or design? None, May had decided.

Wrongly...

And now both her sisters had returned home unexpectedly, and April Robine was in a hotel only a few miles away.

What was she going to do?

Jude was obviously wondering the same thing—if for totally different reasons—as he dropped the kitchen curtain back into place before turning to look at her, dark brows raised mockingly. 'Make your mind up, May,' he drawled. 'Do I go or do I stay?'

She wanted him to go, of course, as far away from here as it was possible for him to go—and for him to take April Robine with him. But as she knew there was no chance of that happening, especially now that Max and Will had arrived, his presence here might be helpful in trying to explain away some of the agitation she was too disturbed to be able to hide.

'You stay,' she told Jude firmly, grasping his arms to sit him down on one of the kitchen chairs. 'Just don't— try not to—' She drew in a deeply controlling breath, willing herself to calm down, knowing that she mustn't make Jude suspicious of her behaviour, either.

What a mess. What an absolute nightmare. What on earth were January and March doing back here? The last time May had spoken to January, she and Max were having such a good time they were staying on in the Caribbean for another week, and had several days to go yet, and March had been nicely ensconced in London meeting her future in-laws. So, if Jude really hadn't told them she was alone here, what were either of them doing back here?

May straightened, forcing herself to calm down.

'Would you please stay, Jude?' she said evenly. 'But could you not—?' She moistened dry lips. 'Please don't mention either David Melton or April Robine's presence in the area?' She looked at him pleadingly, hoping that mentioning David, too, might put him off the scent of it really being the famous actress she didn't want mentioned.

Jude calmly returned her gaze, obviously completely puzzled by her behaviour—but too much a man who liked to be in control, of any situation, to admit to the feeling.

Well, for the moment that would do. Oh, May had no doubts that Jude would demand a more detailed explanation at a later date, but she would deal with that problem when the time came. For the moment she just needed his cooperation over that one point.

He frowned. 'Don't your sisters know about the film offer?'

'Yes, they know about it,' she snapped impatiently. 'They also know that I've turned it down.'

'But not that David Melton is in the area hotly pursuing the subject?' Jude guessed shrewdly.

'No, not that.' May sighed irritably.

'Or that April is here to help press the point. May, what is your problem with April?' he rasped as May felt herself pale just at the mention of the other woman.

She drew in a deeply controlling breath. If he were to mention April Robine in front of her sisters... 'I really would rather not discuss this any more tonight, Jude.' She looked at him determinedly.

Jude's mouth twisted derisively. 'You do realise my silence is going to cost you?' he drawled mockingly.

'Yes,' she sighed her impatience, able to hear the happy murmur of her sisters' voices outside the door now, willing to promise Jude anything right now to ensure his silence concerning April Robine.

'Dinner tomorrow evening?' he prompted softly, obviously also aware of those approaching voices.

May's eyes widened. 'Just dinner?'

Jude frowned darkly, his expression harsh. 'What else did you think I had in mind?' he grated.

'I have no idea,' she dismissed impatiently. 'But dinner tomorrow sounds fine.'

'You don't know how glad I am to hear that!' Jude rasped disgustedly. 'May, I have no idea what sort of man you think I am, but I do not go around—'

'Shh,' she cut in warningly, moving hastily across the room to pick up the coffee-pot as the door began to open, as if she had been in the act of refilling their cups.

The next few minutes were filled with a babble of happy voices as the three sisters greeted each other, January and March absolutely thrilled that their having arrived home unexpectedly as a surprise for May had so obviously worked.

Surprise? May wondered with inward exasperation—her sisters had nearly given her that heart attack Jude had once referred to.

But there was still Jude to introduce to January and March, Max and Will having already greeted their friend, obviously puzzled by his seemingly easy presence here after all the things May had said about him in the past.

'Jude and I ate dinner together while he continued his campaign of trying to talk me into selling the farm,' May breezily explained his presence here to her two future brother-in-laws, deliberately ignoring Max's searching look and Will's puzzled one; the last time she had spoken to either of these men she had made her feelings concerning the absent Jude Marshall perfectly clear, and now here he was, apparently happily ensconced in her kitchen, after having eaten dinner with her.

'Jude can be very persuasive,' Max acknowledged softly.

'Very,' Will echoed dryly.

May turned determinedly away from their two knowing glances. 'January, March, this is Jude Marshall,' she told her sisters more assuredly.

'Jude,' January greeted, shaking his hand guardedly.

'Did you check the food for slow-acting poison before eating?' March, with her usual outspokenness, suffered from no such niceties as she beamed him a mischievous smile.

Jude had stood up as the introductions were made, standing a couple of inches taller even than Max and Will, his sheer physical presence completely dominating. 'I believe you have to be March,' he murmured appreciatively. 'I've heard a lot about both of you,' he explained dryly at March's questioning look. 'As to the poison, I think May and I have what's called a truce at the moment,' he drawled in answer to March's question, at the same time turning to give May a smile that could only be described as intimately loaded.

May's eyes widened, and then she frowned. What on earth was he up to now? Whatever it was, she didn't like it!

'That's great,' Will said with obvious relief.

March nodded as she stood at his side. 'So much better if the best man and the chief bridesmaid don't have any inclination to stab each other part way through the marriage ceremony!' she agreed happily, hazel grey-green eyes sparkling with the mischief that was never far from the surface where March was concerned.

'Best man—'

'Chief bridesmaid—?' May gasped over the top of Jude's own obvious shock.

'Don't look so surprised, you two.' January laughed, obviously a lot happier now than when she had left for her holiday with Max two and a half weeks ago.

For which May was very grateful. January had been very upset after her recent ordeal with a stalker, hence Max's suggestion of a holiday to help her get over it; it seemed to have worked, January absolutely blooming with happiness now.

'Who else would we want as our two main witnesses?' March took up the conversation, grasping both May's hands in hers. 'We thought a double wedding at Easter would be rather fun,' she added encouragingly.

'Very nice,' May assured weakly, very happy for both her sisters, but not so happy at the thought of sharing such a family occasion with Jude Marshall, of all people.

Although it had always been on the cards that would be the case; Jude was obviously an extremely close friend of both Max and Will, their business differences over the buying of this farm apart.

'We would be honoured, wouldn't we, May?' Jude answered for both of them, once again flashing her that intimate smile.

It was a smile, after his recent blackmail into having dinner with him tomorrow evening, that May completely mistrusted.

He was enjoying himself, Jude easily acknowledged. January and March were everything that Max and Will had claimed them to be: absolutely beautiful, charming, with an underlying spark of self-determination that so echoed the one he recognised in May.

It was also interesting to see his hitherto confirmed-bachelor friends so obviously deeply in love with these two beautiful women.

But most of all he was enjoying the fact that for once May was completely disconcerted, that the unexpected arrival of her two sisters had so obviously shaken her. To his eyes, at least. He didn't think that any of the others were aware of it in the same way that he was…

Although there was still the little problem of May having assumed he was behind this surprise arrival of the engaged couples, he acknowledged with a grim tightening of his mouth.

He might be many things, but, despite his previous teasing, he had known all too well that May didn't want either of her sisters told that she was alone here, and, whether he agreed with that decision or not, he had respected it.

'So what brought the four of you back here so unexpectedly?' he prompted casually.

'You mean, because darling May hadn't seen fit to tell any of us that she was managing alone here?' March said dryly with a reproving look at her eldest sister.

Jude gave the middle Calendar sister a look of appreciative respect; obviously these three women had intelligence as well as beauty. Not that he had really doubted that; it would have taken an exceptional woman to attract either Max or Will. It seemed that all three Calendar sisters were that.

May looked uncomfortable at the accusation. 'There was absolutely no reason to tell any of you—'

'But of course there was,' January was the one to cut in concernedly this time, linking her arm with May's as she smiled at her affectionately. 'You can't possibly do all the work here on your own. And to answer your question, Jude—' she turned to him smilingly '—Will telephoned Max on his mobile to tell us the good news about him and March, only to discover that the two of us were still in the Caribbean…' She trailed off with a rueful shrug.

Jude turned to give May a pointed look, receiving an unconvinced glare back.

She really was the most stubborn—

'So, of course we decided to come back immediately,' January said firmly as May would have spoken. 'We met up with March and Will in London, and—'

'Here we all are,' March announced dryly. 'One big happy family.' She looked at Jude with challenging grey-green eyes.

There was a sharpness to March that Jude completely appreciated, easily returning that challenging gaze; Will was certainly going to have his work cut out being married to the middle Calendar sister.

'And we brought champagne to celebrate,' Will put in lightly, obviously not in the least concerned, holding up the two bottles of the bubbly wine he had brought into the house with him.

'March, would you mind helping me get out the champagne glasses?' May prompted briskly, obviously relieved to have something else to do rather than stand around discussing what they had all been doing the last week or so.

Jude having, as he had told May earlier, no siblings of his own, Max and Will had become the brothers Jude had never had, and he was quite happy to spend the next half an hour or so sitting drinking champagne as the six of them toasted everything and everyone, from the newly engaged couples to the best man and chief bridesmaid.

Although he could see by the expression on May's

face that she found the prospect of the latter highly unattractive.

'Look on the positive side, May,' he teased as he moved to stand next to her, shamelessly taking advantage of the situation by slipping his arm lightly about the slenderness of her waist. 'The best man and chief bridesmaid usually partner each other,' he explained. 'Which will save either of us the trouble of having to find someone else to take to the wedding.'

She shot him a quelling glance as he grinned down at her, at the same time wriggling uncomfortably against that restraining arm. 'I'm sure that isn't usually a problem for you, Jude,' she snapped scathingly.

'I was thinking more of you, actually,' he drawled, continuing to grin down at her.

May's cheeks coloured fiery red, and Jude could see by the angry flare in her eyes that she would like to have told him precisely what he could do with his thought.

In fact, she might have just done that, if January hadn't neatly stepped into the conversation. 'You have to see our engagement rings, May.' She laughed. 'Show her, March.' She held out her slender left hand, at the same time that March obligingly did the same.

The two rings were almost identical, an emerald surrounded by slightly smaller diamonds.

'And neither of us knew what the other had chosen until we met up yesterday.' March smiled ruefully.

'What on earth are you doing here?' Max took the opportunity of this distraction to quietly prompt Jude.

Jude gave a shrug, his attention still fixed on the pleasure of the three Calendar women as they admired the engagement rings. 'You knew I was flying over,' he replied as softly.

'But not actually here,' Will joined in the conversation. 'Tell us, did May take a shotgun to you the first time you appeared on the farm?' he added with obvious amusement.

Jude turned to grin at his friend. 'If she had been awake she may just have done that!' he admitted dryly. 'She's certainly fiery enough,' he acknowledged.

Max raised surprised brows. 'May is?' He sounded doubtful.

'May is,' Jude confirmed frowningly; it seemed to him that he and May had done nothing but argue since the moment they'd first met. Or kiss…

'No, that's March,' Will assured him happily. 'May has always been the most reasonable of the three.'

'I agree with you there.' Max nodded slowly, the more serious of the three friends. 'May has always been the easiest of the three sisters.'

Jude gave a firm shake of his head. 'We can't be talking about the same woman,' he assured them dismissively. 'May has been nothing but a pain in the—' He broke off abruptly, the conversation between the three sisters having suddenly ceased, his own voice the only sound to be heard in the otherwise silent kitchen.

'You were saying…?' March arched dark brows at him mischievously, obviously enjoying his discomfort.

And he was discomfited, Jude inwardly acknowledged. It was one thing to say something in confidence to close friends, something else entirely for the subject of the confidence—and her two sisters—to hear what he had said!

And May—the minx—was obviously enjoying his discomfort as much as her sisters were, her mouth twitching with amusement, eyes glowing deeply green.

'Jude?' she prompted with deliberate innocence.

'May—' he gave an exaggerated nod of acknowledgement '—I'm sure that even you would admit that we haven't always—seen eye to eye, since I arrived here?' he derided.

'That could be a little difficult when you're at least eight inches taller than I am,' she returned noncommittally, evoking the laugh from the others that she had obviously hoped for, and breaking the awkwardness of the moment in the process.

At the same time neatly getting Jude out of the tight corner—he admitted it—he had backed himself into.

'Let's drink another toast,' January put in lightly, holding up her glass. 'To a successful wedding.'

'A successful wedding,' Jude echoed with the others, although it was to May that he mockingly saluted his glass, knowing by the narrow-eyed look she gave him in return that she still wasn't happy with the thought of partnering him to the wedding.

He wondered how she would react if he suggested bringing April instead...

CHAPTER EIGHT

'DON'T let us keep you from anything, Jude,' May
prompted firmly a few minutes later, knowing she probably sounded rude, but at the same time wishing him
away from here. With Jude gone, there would be no
chance of April Robine's name being mentioned... 'I'm
sure we all appreciate what a busy man you are, and
Max and Will are obviously staying here tonight,' she
added lightly.

He returned her gaze challengingly for several long
seconds, seemed on the brink of saying something, and
then changed his mind as the tension relaxed from his
shoulders. 'I do have a couple of things to attend to when
I get back to the hotel,' he accepted softly, putting down
his empty champagne glass.

She would just bet he did, May acknowledged tautly,
talking to April Robine—and probably not just talking,
either—being amongst them. 'Then we really mustn't
delay you any longer, must we?' she returned with sac-
charine sweetness.

It was as if there were only the two of them in the
room as their gazes met—and clashed—neither of them
seeming aware of the other four people present as those
gazes continued to war silently.

'Why don't the rest of us go over and see Ginny and
the twins while May and Jude say goodnight?' January
was the one to suggest brightly, putting down her own
empty glass and looking at March and the other two men
expectantly.

'"Ginny and the twins"...?' Max echoed doubtfully even as he prepared to follow her by putting down his own glass.

May smiled at him encouragingly, having taken a great liking to this often overly serious man, knowing that January's warm impetuosity was exactly what he needed to brighten his previously rigid lifestyle.

'It's a female thing,' Jude assured his friend wryly. 'I'll see the two of you some time tomorrow,' he told the two men as they followed their fiancées out of the kitchen.

Leaving May alone with him. Which was the last thing she wanted. But at the same time, she recognised that it was probably necessary; she hadn't finished saying to him earlier all that needed saying, before her sisters and their fiancés had arrived.

'I know. I know.' Jude held up defensive hands as she would have spoken. 'Don't mention David Melton, April Robine, or the film role, to either of your sisters. Did I get that right?' he added tauntingly.

May gave the ghost of a smile. 'You know that you did.' She grimaced. 'It's just that—I don't want—' She broke off awkwardly, shaking her head distractedly.

She couldn't even begin to explain, not to this man, or anyone else. All she knew was that the situation, with the arrival home of her two sisters, had suddenly become so much more complicated. So much so that she just wanted to hide herself away until the danger had passed. And that was something she just couldn't do!

Jude stepped forward, standing very close to her now, looking down at her concernedly as he reached up to caress her cheek. 'Have you never heard that it sometimes helps if you share a problem?' he prompted huskily.

May gave a choked sound, somewhere between a laugh and a sob, she realised heavily. 'Not this problem,' she assured him softly, and certainly not with Jude, of all people. 'They're all so happy, aren't they?' She looked wistfully across towards the barn to where her sisters and their fiancés were no doubt admiring their favourite ewe and her new offspring.

Jude's thumbtips moved beneath her jaw, raising her face so that she was looking directly at him, that grey gaze sharply probing. 'But not you,' he said after a few seconds. 'May, I didn't mean it just now about your being a pain in the—'

'Backside?' she finished ruefully.

'I was going to say proverbial,' he corrected dryly, those thumbtips lightly caressing against her jaw now.

'Yes, you did mean it.' May laughed huskily, wishing he would stop touching her in this way, but feeling powerless to stop him. 'And I know that I have been.' She nodded heavily. 'I just—maybe it would just be better for everyone if we were to sell the farm, after all.' She sighed agitatedly, no longer sure what was the right thing to do. For any of them.

Jude's gaze narrowed. 'You don't really think that,' he said slowly, shaking his head.

'Hey, you're the one that wants to buy it, remember?' she reminded him incredulously. The last thing she had expected was an argument from Jude against her selling the farm.

'So I am.' His mouth twisted ruefully. 'I don't know what I was thinking of,' he added self-disgustedly.

May gave him a searching look. He had seemed different this evening, in the company of his two closest friends, not quite so much the cold-blooded businessman that he usually liked to appear.

She smiled. 'You know, Jude; maybe you aren't such a—'

'Careful, May,' he warned dryly.

'I was going to say hard-headed businessman as I thought you were,' she defended reprovingly.

'Don't you believe it,' he warned hardly. 'Tonight was social.'

She raised dark brows. 'Meaning tomorrow evening will be business?' she taunted.

Jude gave a self-derisive shrug. 'I wouldn't go that far.'

Neither would she. They didn't seem to be able to be in the same room for very long without Jude either kissing or touching her—very disturbing when May had been so determined to keep him at arm's length.

He wasn't at arm's length now, either, standing far too close to her for comfort, those caressing thumbs against her jaw as he lightly cupped her face in gentle hands.

She was falling in love with this man, May realised in sudden shock as she stared up at him.

How on earth had that happened?

With everything else that was going on in her life— David, April Robine's presence in the area, the increasing pressure to sell the farm—how on earth had she managed to fall in love with Jude Marshall, of all people?

His gaze sharpened. 'What is it?' he prompted concernedly. 'You suddenly went pale again,' he explained, frowning darkly.

Pale—she was surprised she hadn't collapsed altogether at the discovery she had just made about herself.

Her lips clamped together as she moved sharply away from him, a shutter coming down over her normally candid gaze. 'I'm tired,' she bit out abruptly, deliberately not looking at him, instead watching as his hands fell ineffectually down by his sides. 'It—I really think you should go now,' she added tautly.

Before she completely lost it. If she hadn't already… Falling in love with Jude Marshall, an obvious friend of her estranged mother's, wasn't exactly a sane thing to do, now was it?

And she was becoming slightly hysterical, May realised shakily. Any minute now she was going to start babbling incoherently, or cry, which was probably worse.

'After all—' her mouth twisted scathingly '—I'm sure April must be expecting you back at the hotel some time tonight.'

Jude's gaze narrowed shrewdly as he seemed to guess her remark had been deliberately antagonising.

But what else could she do? The whole fabric of her life seemed poised in the balance now that she knew she was in love with this man.

Oh, like most women she had her dreams of eventual love and marriage, but in those infrequent day-dreams she had always fallen in love with someone who loved her in return, a kind, caring lover who wanted to love and cherish her for the rest of her life, as she would love and cherish him.

Jude Marshall looked as cherishable as the rogue bull her father had purchased a couple of years ago, before he had had to resell it a few weeks later because of its unmanageability; no one had been able to get near it without the risk of being gored.

Jude was just as untouchable.

He was also the close friend of a woman she would always loathe and despise…

*   *   *

Jude watched May frowningly, the emotions flitting too quickly across her normally candid face to be analysed.

She had also—he knew this without a doubt—just been deliberately rude to him concerning his friendship with April.

April...

If May wouldn't give him the answers he wanted, then perhaps April would. It was worth a try, he decided.

'I'm sure she is,' he lightly answered May's deliberate taunt, determined not to get into yet another argument with her—especially as that seemed to be what she wanted. 'I'll book a table for us somewhere and pick you up about seven-thirty tomorrow evening, okay? May,' he added firmly as she would have spoken, 'when I ask a woman out that's usually exactly what I mean— and that includes calling to collect you in my car,' he added decisively.

She frowned across at him. 'I don't recall there being any asking involved.'

Yes, she was spoiling for yet another fight—and she wasn't going to get one. Not with him, at least.

His mouth thinned determinedly. 'I'll call for you at seven-thirty,' he repeated evenly.

May's derision was obvious as she gave him a scornful smile. 'Effectively ensuring there's no possibility of anyone seeing us out together at your hotel?' she taunted.

Jude drew in a deeply controlling breath before answering her. 'I have no one to hide from, May,' he rasped harshly.

'No?' She raised challenging brows.

He was going to throw caution to the wind in a minute, go back on his earlier decision, and kiss the life out of her—something guaranteed to result in another fight.

'Your father should have smacked your bottom more when you were a child,' he bit out tautly, his hands clenched at his sides as he fought the urge to take her in his arms.

She gave a wistful shake of her head. 'My father didn't believe in physical punishment for any of his children.'

'Making their husband's role all the more difficult!' he dismissed hardly.

May's smile deepened. 'Max and Will don't seem to have any complaints.'

'Yet,' he scorned.

Her smile faded as suddenly as it had appeared. 'Ever,' she snapped with certainty. 'January and March are both lovely young women—'

'Aren't you just the teeniest bit prejudiced?' Jude derided, knowing he had her rattled now with what she saw as criticism of her sisters.

'And isn't your nose just the teeniest bit out of joint because your two closest friends are about to get married and break up the bachelor threesome?' she returned challengingly.

Jude drew in a sharp breath. Not out of anger. Not out of indignation. But because a part of him knew that she was right...

He had been friends with Max and Will for years, the three men often spending huge chunks of time together, playing hard as well as working hard. It was a little unsettling to realise, with Max and Will's recent engagements, the pending marriages, that time was now over.

And he didn't thank May for bringing his attention to the fact.

'Doesn't that idiom, considering your obvious closeness to your two sisters, apply equally well to you?' he taunted, instantly wishing his words unsaid as May paled, telling him that his taunt had hit its mark. 'This is getting us nowhere, May,' he dismissed, moving away impatiently. 'Whatever it is you're trying to do with this conversation, I refuse to play. Okay?' he added hardly, aware of how he had nearly completely lost his temper.

Something that never happened. As May had so acutely guessed from the beginning, he gave little of himself away, either verbally or emotionally, something that anger was guaranteed to do.

Except that May Calendar seemed able to get under that barrier he had deliberately erected about his emotions, seemingly without any effort whatsoever…

'I have no idea what you're talking about,' she dismissed, moving across to the kitchen window. 'They're all coming back now, so—'

'It's time for me to leave,' he finished impatiently. 'May, considering the favour I'm doing you—not mentioning Melton or April,' he explained at her questioning look, 'you could be a little politer to me than you've been the last few minutes.'

Her mouth twisted humourlessly. 'I'm afraid you don't bring out that quality in me,' she drawled. 'Any more than I bring it out in you,' she added pointedly. 'Now, if you wouldn't mind, I have some beds to make up for my unexpected guests…'

Jude's gaze narrowed. 'You—'

'Still here, Jude?' March Calendar mocked as she was the first of the quartet to enter the kitchen. 'We thought you would have left long ago.'

'Then you thought wrong, didn't you?' Jude bit out irritably; another Calendar sister who needed her backside smacked. 'Max, would you mind walking out to my car with me?' he prompted lightly.

'No problem,' his friend dismissed, turning to give January a lingering kiss on the lips before following Jude from the farmhouse.

This was certainly going to take some getting used to, Jude realised ruefully as the two men walked over to his hire car; Max had always been more of the loner of the three men, enjoying relationships but never allowing any female to get too close to him. Obviously that had all changed with his obvious love for January Calendar. No doubt Will was as entranced by March.

'They're quite something, aren't they?' Max drawled ruefully as he seemed to guess at least some of Jude's thoughts.

But not all of them, thank goodness—because Jude had just come to the startling conclusion that, if he weren't very careful, he could end up as bewitched by May Calendar as his two friends were by her sisters.

How the hell had *that* happened?

When had it happened?

More to the point, *why* had it happened? The last thing he needed, the last thing he wanted, was to fall in love with any woman, let alone one as prickly as May was turning out to be.

'Jude?' Max prompted concernedly.

He gave his friend a startled look, realising Max was still waiting for an answer to his casual statement. Casual to Max, that was. That was the last thing it was to Jude.

'Quite something,' he acknowledged hardly. 'Although I didn't really bring you out here to talk about the Calendar sisters,' he added harshly.

'You didn't?' Max leant back against the hire car.

'You and May seemed to be getting along just fine when we all arrived,' he added speculatively.

'Don't start,' Jude warned, eyes glinting silver. Max and Will were probably the only two people who really knew him well, and the last thing he wanted was for either of them to get the idea he was interested in May in anything but a business way. 'I want to buy this farm from her,' he rasped. 'I would hardly be rude to her.'

Max shrugged. 'That's never stopped you being rude to people in the past.'

'You—' Jude couldn't help himself—he laughed. 'You're right.' He nodded, still grinning ruefully. 'But May's been having a hard time of it managing here on her own.' He shrugged. 'I—I felt sorry for her.'

Max's eyes widened at the admission.

As well they might, Jude accepted irritably. Feeling sorry for people he was trying to beat in business had never been part of his make-up, either. But it was better that Max think that than to have the other man guess how confused Jude's emotions had really become where May was concerned. So confused he didn't know what they were himself any more.

'Not that she would thank me for the sentiment,' he continued derisively. 'The woman had more spikes than a hedgehog!'

Max laughed appreciatively. 'So if you didn't want to talk about the Calendar sisters, what did you bring me out here for?'

Jude straightened. 'You remember April, of course?' he prompted guardedly, knowing that the other man did; they had both become friends of April's while in America.

'Of course.' Max nodded. 'How did it go with her after I left the States—?'

'She's here,' Jude cut in decisively. 'At the hotel. Oh, not staying with me,' he added impatiently as Max's expression turned to one of speculation. 'She had some business of her own to do over here, so we travelled over together, that's all— What the hell are you looking at me like that for?' he demanded as Max raised questioning brows.

'Like what?' Max returned innocently.

'Oh, never mind.' Jude felt too irritable, too disquieted altogether, to be able to deal with this right now. 'The thing is that May has taken some sort of instant dislike to her— You're doing it again!' he snapped as Max once again looked speculative.

Max shrugged. 'April is a very beautiful woman—'

'The way April looks has nothing to do with May's dislike of her; as far as I can tell she disliked her before the two of them even met.' He sighed his impatience.

'Interesting,' Max murmured slowly.

'Interesting or not, all I want from you is a promise not to mention April's name in the Calendar home. Don't ask.' He sighed again as Max looked more puzzled than ever. 'I have yet to get to the bottom of that particular story, but when I do I'll let you know, okay?'

'Okay.' Max shrugged, straightening. 'Say hello to April for me,' he added as Jude got into the car.

'Will do.' He nodded before driving away, hoping that Max wouldn't see his hurried departure for what it really was.

Escaping from May and the confusion of emotions that suddenly went with her...

CHAPTER NINE

'I WANT to know exactly what you told Jude last night,' May stated flatly.

'And a good morning to you, too, May,' April Robine returned dryly, perfectly composed as she moved to sit in the chair opposite May's in the hotel lounge, looking as beautiful as ever in a tailored black dress that showed off the perfection of her figure and long, slender legs.

May continued to scowl; she hadn't come here to exchange pleasantries with this woman.

In fact, she wished she didn't have to be here at all, but in the circumstances of her having dinner with Jude this evening she really needed to know what he knew.

'It's raining outside,' she dismissed uninterestedly. 'And I repeat, what did you tell Jude last night?'

'You know, May,' April said consideringly, her head tilted to one side, 'your manners were better at five years old than they are now!'

May felt the warmth of colour enter her cheeks, the barb hitting home in spite of herself. She had been brought up with impeccable manners—they all had; they just seemed to have gone out of the window since the advent of Jude Marshall and April Robine into her life.

'When Reception informed me you were waiting to see me downstairs, I ordered coffee for us both. Thank you.' April turned to smile at the waitress as she arrived with the coffee tray. 'I hope you don't mind?' she prompted May lightly as she sat forward to pour the aromatic brew.

'You go ahead,' May invited stiffly once they were alone again. 'I had a coffee before leaving home.' And she certainly hadn't come here to spend a sociable half-hour with this woman.

'It won't choke you to have coffee with me, you know, May,' April said tautly, eyes flashing deeply green.

May gave a barely perceptible shake of her head as she recognised that angry characteristic in the other woman as one of her own. In fact, apart from the length of their hair, and the obvious difference in their ages, the similarities between the two women were so notice-able, to May at least, that she was surprised no one else—namely David or Jude—had put two and two to-gether and come up with the appropriate answer of four.

But it was only a matter of time...

'That's a matter of opinion,' she snapped dismis-sively. 'I only want to know—'

'What I told Jude last night,' April finished dryly. 'And my answer to that is, why should I have told Jude anything, last night or any other time?'

This wasn't going to be as easy as she had thought it would be, May realised heavily. The last thing she had wanted to do was come here and talk to this woman at all, but she really had felt that she had no choice in the matter; Jude was already far too superior in his manner for her liking—if April were to tell him of their family connection then the whole situation would become un-bearable.

As it was May had found it very difficult to continue to act normally with her two sisters and their fiancés after Jude's departure the previous evening, knowing Jude was intelligent enough to realise that if she wouldn't give him any answers to his questions his only other source of information was April...

She gave an impatient movement of her hand. 'Because Jude knows there's something going on—he just doesn't know what it is. At least, he didn't...' she added pointedly.

April poured coffee into the second cup, adding the cream before placing it on the table in front of May. 'I take it you still don't like sugar in hot drinks?' she prompted huskily.

No, she still didn't like sugar in hot drinks—but it was completely disturbing to realise that this woman remembered her well enough to know that...!

'Miss Robine—'

'April,' the older woman cut in tersely. 'If you can't call me anything else, then call me April,' she added firmly as May looked at her frowningly.

Call her anything else...? What sort of 'anything else' did the other woman have in mind? Surely not 'Mother'.

May nodded abruptly. 'April,' she ground out tersely. 'I don't want any coffee. I don't want to exchange polite pleasantries. I just want—'

'To know what I said to Jude last night,' the other woman repeated heavily. 'But as I haven't seen Jude since we all met at the farm together yesterday evening, I have no idea why you think I have told him anything.'

May's eyes widened. April hadn't seen Jude again last night...? Could Jude possibly be telling the truth when he denied having any sort of intimate relationship with the beautiful actress? It was incredible if that really were the case, but as they both denied that such a relationship existed—

What difference did it make in the huge scheme of

things? Jude's friendship with April alone was enough to make him a danger to the harmony of her family.

Although May couldn't deny the small surge of warmth inside her at the knowledge that the man she loved wasn't involved with the woman who had been her mother. Not that she thought her own feelings for him were going anywhere, either, but it would make those feelings unbearable if she knew he was intimately involved with April.

'Did something happen, May?' April prompted frowningly. 'Have you and Jude argued—?'

'Jude and I have done nothing but argue since the moment we first met. In fact, before we first met.' She grimaced.

'Explain that last remark, please.' April frowned.

May sighed. What difference did it make if April knew about the farm? It was absolutely none of this woman's business, but at the same time it really didn't matter if she knew; April's own interest in the farm—if she had ever had one—had ended long ago.

May shrugged. 'Jude wants to buy the farm.'

April looked surprised. 'What on earth for?'

'The reasons aren't important; the farm isn't for sale.'

'But—'

'It isn't for sale,' May repeated firmly, her own eyes flashing a warning now.

Two pairs of identical green eyes warred for several long seconds before April gave a puzzled sigh. 'Okay, Jude wants to buy the farm, you don't want to sell; are you trying to tell me that's the only involvement between the two of you?'

'Of course that's the only involvement between the two of us,' May assured her impatiently. 'Do I look like the type of woman Jude Marshall would be romantically interested in?' she added disgustedly.

April sat back in her chair, looking at May consideringly now. 'And why shouldn't he be interested in you?' she finally said slowly. 'You're beautiful. Intelligent. A very talented actress, according to David,' she added ruefully. 'So why shouldn't Jude be attracted to you?'

'Never mind,' May dismissed impatiently.

'But—'

'My only interest in Jude is what you may or may not have told him about our own—connection,' May cut in determinedly.

'Nothing,' April snapped. 'Absolutely nothing,' she repeated tightly. 'And I presume you want it to continue that way?' She arched dark brows.

'Most definitely,' May scorned. 'And I don't want you coming to the farm again, either,' she added hardly.

Pain flickered across the beautiful features so well known to film and television viewers alike, the eyes now a dark, unfathomable green. 'You really hate me, don't you?' April choked.

'How I do or don't feel about you really isn't important,' May dismissed impatiently. 'January and March arrived back home unexpectedly last night, and—'

'January and March are here, too?' April breathed huskily, eyes wide, her beautiful face lit with anticipation.

May scowled her displeasure at the other woman's response to this information. 'You're dead, remember,' she stated flatly.

The other woman flinched as if May had physically struck her, all the colour fading from her cheeks, the deep red lipgloss she wore standing out in stark contrast to that paleness.

'You enjoyed saying that.' April winced, putting up a hand to cover the emotional quiver of her lips.

May felt a momentary guilt at April's obvious pain, but it was a guilt she quickly squashed as she remembered this woman's abandonment of her husband and three young daughters. After all, this woman was the one who had left them, not the other way around. And she really couldn't expect that any of them would want to see her again now.

'You're wrong, I'm not enjoying any of this situation,' May assured her emphatically. 'It just happens to be fact.' She shrugged. 'You—'

'How did your father explain the money?' April cut in frowningly. 'What did he tell you all? That there was a rich uncle around somewhere who liked to help out occasionally?'

May looked at the other woman for several long seconds, and then she turned to rummage through her handbag, finding what she was looking for almost immediately. 'I called at the bank before coming here this morning,' she told April woodenly. 'I wanted to be able to give you this.' She held out the piece of paper in her hand.

April's hand visibly trembled as she reached out to take the paper, that trembling increasing as she looked down at the cheque May had given her.

'It's all there,' May told her evenly. 'Including the interest.'

Tears swam in the pained green eyes as April looked up at her. 'He didn't use any of it,' she groaned. 'Not a single penny.'

It had been the shock of May's life when, on the death of her father, she had been informed of the money in his bank accounts, one that was used for the everyday expenses, and predictably contained very little, a second one that contained a few hundred pounds her father had saved for a rainy day, and a third that contained an amount of money that made May's eyes widen incredulously. Until informed by the bank manager that an amount was placed in that account every month, increasingly so, and had been for the last twenty years. It had been the almost twenty years that had given it away; after that it hadn't taken too much intelligence to work out who could have been making those payments…

'No, he didn't,' May confirmed huskily. 'Did you really think that he would?' She gave a pained frown.

April swallowed hard. 'I—I hoped that he would. I—wanted you girls to have things, pretty things—'

'Why?' May laughed humourlessly. 'Did you really think that ''things'' could make it up to us for not having a mother?' She shook her head incredulously. 'I'm glad my father didn't use any of that money, I would have been disappointed in him if he had.'

The amount in the account was an absolute fortune, could have made all of their lives so much easier, but May knew very well why her father had refused to use it, even to ease the lives of his daughters as they grew up. For the same reason May had refused to touch a penny of it since he had died…

'You're so like him.' April spoke huskily now, shaking her head slightly. 'You look like me, but you're so like your father—'

'I'm glad of that,' May said with satisfaction, but nevertheless the barb—if indeed that was what it had been meant as—hit home; this woman believed her to be like the man she hadn't been able to stay married to, to the point that she had left her children in order to escape him.

But her father had been a good man, an honest man. Not always able to show his affection, perhaps, but none of his daughters had ever doubted his love for them. As May had never doubted that he had continued to love the wife who had left him until the day he'd died...

'Believe it or not, so am I,' April choked emotionally. 'Are January and March like him, too? Do they—?'

'I absolutely refuse to discuss them with you,' May cut in coldly, hands clenched angrily in her lap. 'You—'

'Well, hello, ladies,' interrupted a silkily familiar voice. 'Having another one of your cosy little chats?' Jude prompted lightly as he came to stand beside the table they sat at.

Cosy hardly described the chat between the two women, May fumed angrily, wondering how much of their conversation Jude had overheard before interrupting them, turning to glare up at him suspiciously, only to have that angry gaze met with by one of bland indifference. Whatever Jude might or might not have overheard he wasn't about to give any of that away from his expression.

But April, May was at least relieved to see, had had the foresight to push the cheque she had just given her away in her own handbag. Away from curious eyes...

'I telephoned the farm earlier, but neither January nor March had any idea where you were,' Jude informed May as he sat down at the table with them without being invited.

May stared at him impotently, once again having that feeling that this whole situation was rolling away from her...

Jude continued to look at May for several seconds, but could gauge very little from her expression. She was getting as good at this as he was himself.

It had been quite a surprise to see May chatting away with April when he'd stepped out of the lift a few minutes ago, the two of them looking intensely serious about something. He had considered—briefly—not interrupting them, but on second thoughts had decided the opportunity of talking to the two of them together was too good to miss.

'Why were you trying to find me?' May spoke sharply, her voice husky, as if she were finding it difficult to talk at all.

Jude relaxed back in his chair, his expression deliberately inscrutable. 'I wasn't. I actually telephoned to talk to Max, but March seemed to assume it was you I wanted to talk to, and before I could correct her on the matter she had explained that neither she nor your sister had any idea where you were.'

May's mouth firmed at this disclosure. 'I can see I will have to ask my sisters to be a little more—circumspect, in what they tell complete strangers about my movements!'

In spite of himself, Jude felt some of his inscrutability slip at her deliberately insulting tone, knowing it was what she wanted but unable to stop the tightening of his mouth and the narrowing of his eyes. She really was—

'Max?' April repeated lightly, drawing his attention to her and away from May. 'Is Max here, too?' She smiled delightedly.

'He is.' Jude nodded ruefully. 'And he's now engaged to marry one of May's sisters,' he explained dryly, no longer looking at May but nevertheless aware—if puzzled—by the way she had stiffened as April's comment revealed that she obviously knew Max, too.

'How lovely,' April said with genuine delight, her eyes glowing deeply green. 'March or January?' she prompted interestedly.

'January, as it happens,' May was the one to answer curtly. 'Although I can't see what difference it makes to you which one it is,' she added disgruntledly.

April looked flustered. 'Well…no. But—' she gave an impatient shake of her head before turning to smile at Jude '—I'm so pleased for Max,' she told him huskily.

So was Jude, well aware of the reason for Max's previous determination never to fall in love, pleased that someone as beautiful and charming as January Calendar had managed to overcome Max's barriers.

But it was May's reaction to April's acquaintance with Max that intrigued him…

Jude nodded. 'We'll have to arrange for us all to have dinner together one—'

'No!' May gasped protestingly, although she seemed to regret the protest as soon as she had made it, a shutter coming down over her eyes even as her face paled.

Jude gave her a quizzical glance. 'I didn't mean this evening,' he drawled mockingly, having no intention of anyone intruding on his evening with May. As seemed to have happened every other time he had tried to spend time alone with her.

'I didn't think you did,' May snapped dismissively, obviously not in the least concerned with that. 'But I'm sure Miss Robine is far too busy for socialising on that scale,' she added with what looked like a pointed glare in April's direction.

April returned that glare, neither woman seeming aware of Jude's presence as the silent war of wills continued for several long seconds.

Giving Jude time to study them unobserved. They

were both such lovely women, inside as well as out, that it was totally unbelievable to him that the two of them didn't even like each other. Well…no, that wasn't strictly accurate; April seemed to like May well enough, it was May who was so antagonistic.

What could she possibly have against someone as charmingly gracious as April—?

Jude froze in his seat, his gaze suddenly fixed as he looked at the two women, the expressions of determination on their faces absolutely identical. In fact, apart from the twenty or so years' difference in their ages, the two faces bore a striking resemblance to each other…

What?

His gaze narrowed as he studied the two women more closely, noting the ebony hair, the creamy brow, deep green eyes, the generously kissable mouth, pointed determination of the chin, the slender curvaceousness of the body.

My God…!

Apart from the difference in their ages, these two women might have been sisters. But as they couldn't possibly be sisters, that only left—

But it couldn't be!

Could it…?

CHAPTER TEN

'YOU know, don't you?' May said huskily, her gaze not quite meeting Jude's.

She had been dreading seeing him again this evening, ever since this morning at the hotel when she had finally broken her gaze from April Robine's to turn and see Jude looking at the two of them as if he had just been punched between his eyes—or that he couldn't quite believe what his eyes had been undoubtedly telling him. Except, May was sure by the shutter that had suddenly come down over those silver-grey pools, that he had believed it…

But after that first shocked reaction, he had continued to chat quite amiably with the two women, obviously had had no intention of going anywhere, leaving it to May to have been the one to make her departure, knowing there had been nothing further she could do there that morning. In fact, if what she suspected concerning Jude was true, she had probably made things worse.

And so she had left the hotel, totally distracted as she'd carried out the work on the farm for the rest of the day, picking up the telephone in the hallway at least half a dozen times with the intention of cancelling their dinner engagement for this evening, only to have put it down again as she'd accepted that she would only have been delaying the inevitable. Besides, there was always the possibility—more than a possibility—that Jude had questioned April once May had left the hotel…

His expression had been unreadable when he'd arrived

120

at the farm to pick May up at exactly seven-thirty, looking extremely handsome in a dark business suit, grey shirt, and neatly knotted tie, receiving raised-brow looks from both Max and Will as they'd helped January and March prepare their own dinner, although neither man had actually made any comment about the fact that Jude and May had obviously been going out to dinner together.

May had chosen her own clothes carefully for this evening, not wanting to give the impression she'd thought she was actually going out on a date with Jude—which she most certainly wasn't—but at the same time needing to look a bit more glamorous than she usually did. If only to give her more confidence than she'd actually felt. The fitted dark green above-knee-length dress, teamed with a contrasting black jacket, had seemed about right to her.

Although she hadn't been quite so sure of that when they'd arrived at the French restaurant where Jude had booked them a table for the evening, having heard of its exclusivity, of course, but never having even contemplated coming here herself; a farmer's income didn't stretch to frequenting places like this.

Jude had been chattily polite on the drive here, very solicitous as they'd been seated at their table, consulting her on her preference to wine before ordering. But to May that had all been just delaying the inevitable, and now that they had ordered their food, the wine had been opened and poured, she knew she couldn't delay any longer.

'Jude?' she prompted softly when he didn't answer her earlier comment. 'Did you—did you talk to April once I left this morning?' She couldn't exactly blame him if he had; from the look of stunned disbelief she had seen on his face this morning he had a lot of questions he needed answers to.

'Well, of course I talked to April once you had left this morning; it would have been rude not to,' he drawled dismissively, sipping his wine. 'What do you think of this?' He held up his glass. 'Is it dry enough for you—?'

'It's fine,' May dismissed impatiently, not having even tasted it, but sure that it was going to be as perfect as everything else about this tastefully decorated and efficiently run restaurant. 'Would you stop avoiding the issue, Jude, and just—?' She broke off, drawing in a deep breath, closing her eyes briefly before looking across at him. 'You do know, don't you, Jude.' It was a statement this time rather than a question.

He grimaced, leaning forward to put down his wineglass before answering. 'I—damn it, May, how can it be possible?' He frowned darkly. 'You're—April is—' He made an impatient movement with his hand.

'Yes?' May prompted softly, almost feeling sorry for him as she sensed his confusion, his disbelief.

He gave an abrupt shake of his head. 'Even if you hadn't told me so yourself, Max and Will have both informed me, on separate occasions, that both your parents are dead,' he said exasperatedly.

'They are,' she confirmed abruptly.

Jude gave a decisive shake of his head now. 'We both know that isn't true,' he rasped. 'May, my eyes weren't deceiving me this morning—'

'I never implied for a moment that there is anything wrong with your eyesight,' May assured him dryly.

'Then we both know that April is your mo—'

'She gave up the right to that title twenty-two years

ago when she walked out on her husband and three small daughters,' May cut in harshly.

'So it is true,' Jude breathed softly, looking totally stunned now, as if, despite what he had already said, he hadn't quite been able to believe his own suspicions until that moment of confirmation.

May picked up her glass and took a sip of her wine, giving Jude the time he needed to collect his thoughts, but at the same time giving herself some Dutch courage; this was turning out to be more traumatic than she had even imagined.

'You didn't ask April?' May couldn't keep the surprise out of her voice; the pair seemed to be such friends, it had seemed logical to her that he would have talked to the other woman about his suspicions.

'Of course I didn't ask April!' Jude rasped impatiently, sitting forward to once again pick up his wineglass and take a much-needed swallow of the white wine. 'I told you, we don't have the sort of close friendship that would allow me to intrude on her private life in that way.'

'But you think we have?' she derided with a disbelieving smile.

His eyes glittered silver. 'I didn't bring the subject up, May—you did,' he reminded hardly.

She gave a shrug. 'We could hardly have spent the whole evening together and totally ignored the subject.'

'Not with any comfort, no,' he accepted heavily. 'But if you had chosen not to mention it, I doubt that I would have, either. I'm totally at a loss to understand any of it, May,' he continued agitatedly as she would have spoken. 'And, as I'm sure you're totally aware, that isn't something I admit to lightly,' he added self-derisively.

'No.' May gave a rueful smile.

'Do January and March know their mother is still alive?' he prompted softly.

May's smile faded. 'No,' she said hardly. 'And I don't want them to know, either.' And for that to happen, she now had to ask for this man's cooperation. Something she wasn't sure he would give... 'How do you think they would both feel if they were to be told the truth now? How would you feel?' she reasoned impatiently.

'But it isn't me, May,' he came back explosively. 'It isn't you, either, not really—'

'Of course it is—'

'No.' He gave a slow shake of his head at her angry outburst. 'If my guess is correct, and from what I've observed the last few days, then you've always known your mother was still alive, it's January and March who have lived in ignorance of the fact. And maybe that was the right thing to do at the time, I don't know.' He gave a baffled grimace. 'But do you really think, now that April is here, in England, only ten miles or so away, that you have the right to keep that information from your sisters any longer?'

May bit back her own angry retort as their first courses were delivered to the table, still silent once they had been left alone once again.

Because the truth of the matter was, she wasn't sure herself any more that she had that right.

Oh, she had never doubted the rightness of what she'd been doing as they'd all been growing up, had known that it was easier for everyone—but especially their father—if questions about the mother the two younger sisters barely remembered were kept to a minimum. Which they wouldn't have been if either January or March had realised their mother was still alive, was now a successful actress living in America.

But these last few weeks, since May had been offered the role in a film playing the part of April Robine's daughter, had been something of a strain, made even more so because of David Melton's persistence in trying to get her to accept the part.

And she didn't welcome Jude putting into words the question that had been plaguing her the last few weeks, but especially so since April Robine had arrived on the scene.

With Jude, of all people…

Jude watched the emotions flitting across May's expressive face, knew that he had hit a raw nerve with his last question.

But what else could he do? Now that May had actually confirmed what he had only suspected this morning, he felt he had no choice but to play the devil's advocate. Which was guaranteed to make May hate him all the more.

If that were possible…

'She's the reason you turned down the offer of the film role, isn't she?' Jude realised shrewdly. 'You were trying to avoid something like this happening.'

'Can you blame me?' May's eyes flashed angrily.

She was hurting, he could see she was hurting, and he wanted nothing more at that moment than to take her in his arms, assure her that everything was going to be okay, that it would all work itself out.

But the former he didn't think she would accept at all, and he wasn't sure the latter were true.

How did you set about telling two grown women of twenty-six and twenty-five that the mother you had told them was dead was actually very much alive and staying in a hotel ten miles away?

Worse, how was May going to stop April telling January and March the truth, if that was what she chose to do? If they needed any telling after meeting the actress face to face, that was.

He now knew that it was April that May had reminded him of the first day he'd come to the farm. Despite the fact that the women were such a contrast to each other, April always chicly elegant, May dressed in overbig clothes that day, an unattractive woollen hat pulled over her hair, there had still been enough of a likeness between the two women for Jude to have felt a jolt of something. He just hadn't known what that something was until this morning...

'I'm not the one you have to worry about blaming you for anything, May,' he told her gently. 'It's January and March you have to convince of that.'

He wished the words unsaid almost as soon as he had said them, May's face paling dramatically, her eyes huge green pools of pain in that paleness.

He put out a comforting hand, the sudden anger that flared in her eyes stopping him from actually touching her; she was so tense now she looked as if the merest touch might shatter her.

'I might have known this would be your attitude,' she snapped scornfully, her hands tightly gripping the napkin spread on her lap. 'It must be so easy to sit in judgement, in the total security of being an only child of obviously caring parents. But you can have no idea of what it was like when—when April left us the way she did. No idea.' She was fighting back the tears now, obviously determined to remain in control.

That was May's problem, Jude realised achingly; she had always been the eldest sister—by one year, for goodness' sake—the one who took all the problems of the family on board and sorted them out for all of them. But who sorted out May's problems...?

He shook his head. 'It's too big a burden for you to carry alone any more, May—'

'And who's going to help me?' she cut in tauntingly. 'You? Somehow I don't think so.' She looked at him scornfully.

Jude schooled himself not to react to that scorn, knowing that May was hurting very badly at this moment, that, no matter what she might say to the contrary, she must be filled with doubts as to the rightness of her own actions in keeping the truth from her two sisters. Or else she wasn't the warmly caring woman he thought she was...

He shrugged. 'I would help, if I could, and if you would let me—which you obviously won't,' he accepted dryly before she could speak. 'But I was thinking more along the lines of April—'

'Oh, please!' she cut in scathingly. 'April is the last person I want help from!'

Once again Jude held back his initial response to this scornful remark; losing his own temper wasn't going to help this situation at all. Besides, May was agitated enough for both of them.

There was also the factor that they were sitting in a crowded restaurant, the tables not particularly close together, but close enough that several people had already glanced their way when their voices had become slightly louder than was normal; this really wasn't the place for this conversation to take place.

'Let's eat, hmm,' he suggested softly, picking up his own knife and fork in preparation of eating the gravid lax he had ordered. 'Most things look better on a full stomach,' he added as May made no move to do likewise with her garlic prawns.

She continued to look mutinous for several long seconds, but a glance around the restaurant, where several people still seemed to be casting them curious looks, was enough to convince her of the rightness of the action.

Not that there was much chance of May achieving a full stomach on the amount of food she ate, merely picking at the prawns, and pushing uninterestedly about the plate the chicken she had ordered to follow. As for conversation, that was almost nonexistent, Jude wary of introducing any subject that was going to tip May over the edge of the tight control she had over herself, and May herself not in the least conversational.

Not the most successful of evenings, Jude acknowledged as May refused dessert but ordered a cup of strong black coffee to finish off their meal.

'May—'

'I don't wish to discuss this with you any more, Jude,' she snapped warningly, eyes flashing deeply green.

So like April's, Jude realised with that dazed feeling that was becoming so familiar to him.

Why hadn't he seen the likeness between the two women sooner?

What difference did it make when he discovered the likeness? he instantly chided himself. He had realised it now. That was the real problem, wasn't it…?

What would May have done if he had never seen the similarity between the two women? Would she simply have persuaded April to go away quietly? Or something else? Because he had a feeling, whether May liked it or not, that April's days of 'going away quietly' were over.

He had seen the look of excited anticipation on April's face this morning just at the mention of January and

March, could easily see that, having now met May, April would want to meet her other two daughters, too.

Something May was totally against.

He drew in a deep breath. 'Whether you like it or not, May, you're going to have to discuss this situation with someone.'

'Why am I?' she challenged hardly.

The uneasy truce they had come to during their meal was obviously at an end, Jude accepted ruefully. 'Because you are,' he reasoned softly. 'May, April isn't going to disappear just because it's what you want her to do—'

'Why isn't she?' May put in sharply.

He gave a weary shake of his head. 'You're doing it again, May. Answering a question with a question,' he explained at her enquiring look. 'No matter how much you might want to do so, May, you can't keep running away from this situation—'

'I'm not running away from anything!' she defended heatedly.

He grimaced. 'It certainly looks that way from where I'm sitting.'

'Does it really?' she bit out scornfully. 'Well, you're totally wrong about that. Just as you're totally wrong about what I can or can't do,' she assured him with hard dismissal, throwing her napkin down on the table-top before standing up. 'And what I want to do right now is walk out of here and go home—'

'I drove you here,' he protested impatiently.

'Then I'll get a taxi,' she told him uncaringly, picking up her bag and walking out of the restaurant, glancing neither left nor right as she went, intent only on leaving.

Jude stared after her frustratedly, at the same time aware that several other people in the restaurant had watched May's obviously stormy departure with interest, watching curiously now to see if he would follow her.

Not that he was in the least interested in what other people thought, about him, or anyone he was with, for that matter. It was May that concerned him now.

And, damn it, he didn't want to be concerned about her. Didn't want to be concerned about any woman to the extent that May Calendar had got under his skin.

Because he could no longer deny that she had done that, completely, and, he was very much afraid, irretrievably.

Which left him precisely where?

Following May out of the restaurant, that was where that left him, he acknowledged begrudgingly even as he stood up to pay the bill and hurry outside in pursuit of her.

CHAPTER ELEVEN

WHY was there never, ever, a taxi around when you wanted one? May wondered emotionally as she stood on the pavement looking up and down the road, tears of frustration blurring her vision.

She should have known Jude wouldn't help her, should have known that he would take April's part in all this. She didn't know what she had been thinking of even considering appealing to his caring instinct—Jude Marshall didn't have a caring instinct in the whole of his body, had only invited her out this evening at all because he still intended to buy the farm. He—

'Get in the car, May,' Jude instructed through the open window of the car he had just parked on the road in front of her.

'I would rather walk the whole way home than get in a car, or anything else, with you!' she assured him emotionally, hurriedly wiping away the tell-tale tears with the knuckles of her hands as she turned away with the intention of doing just that.

Jude swung out of the driver's side of the car, slamming the door behind him before walking round to where May faced him so defiantly. 'Do all three of you have some sort of death wish?' Jude rasped angrily even as he grasped her arm and swung her round to face him. 'First January is involved with some sort of stalker,' he enlarged at her outraged expression. 'And now you're contemplating walking the ten miles home, at eleven o'clock at night, along roads that are so dark an attacker could be hiding behind every bush.' He gave a disgusted shake of his head.

May stared up at him in the light from the street-lamp overhead. 'An attacker behind every bush'? What sort of area did he think this was? This wasn't London. Or one of the other crowded cities. This was a quiet little backwater in the north of England—

And only weeks ago there had been a stalker in the area, someone who had taken pleasure in beating up women.

But he had been caught, May instantly derided her own thoughts; what were the chances of there being a second person like that in an area this uninhabited?

She shook her head. 'I'll find a taxi along the way,' she assured him dismissively.

Jude's mouth thinned. 'Get in the car, May.' There was no menace in his voice, just flat fury, his eyes glittering silver in the lamplight as he opened the passenger door for her to get in.

She looked up at him frustratedly. 'You're overreacting, Jude—'

'*I'm* overreacting?' he repeated explosively. 'You just walked out on me in the middle of our meal in a crowded restaurant—'

'The coffee stage is hardly the middle of a meal, Jude,' May cut in impatiently.

His hand tightened painfully on her arm. 'May, so far this has been far from the most enjoyable evening of my life, I am not going to add returning to the hotel, only to worry about your safety for the next couple of hours, to the list of things that went wrong with this evening.'

She glared up at him frustratedly, knowing him well enough to realise that if she did start to walk home, he was quite capable of following slowly along beside her in his car all the way back to the farm. Put like that, she might as well be warm and comfortable inside the car...

'All right,' she conceded forcefully. 'But I do not want to discuss April Robine any more tonight.'

He arched dark brows. 'May, do you really think you're in any position at this point to attach conditions?' he muttered impatiently.

The passenger door to the car stood open; Jude was obviously much bigger and stronger than she was, perfectly capable of pushing her inside the vehicle whether she wanted to go or not, in fact. And yet she somehow didn't think he would do that...

Her mouth set stubbornly. 'You agree not to discuss April Robine, or I don't get in the car.'

He gave a frustrated sigh. 'All right,' he snapped harshly. 'Just get in, will you?' he added wearily.

May gave him a long considering look before turning to get inside the passenger side of car, determined not to talk to him at all unless she absolutely had to—they had both said too much already this evening.

Luckily, Jude seemed disinclined to talk, either, driving in stony silence, the journey seeming to take twice as long to May because of the obvious tension between the two of them.

But what else could Jude have expected? He was treading on ground he had no business trespassing on.

Even if he had realised April Robine's connection to her family, a little voice taunted her.

Yes, even then. Because it was family business, concerned the four women involved, and no one else. No matter what Jude might think to the contrary.

'Thank you,' she told him stiltedly once he had parked the car in the farmyard some time later.

Jude turned off the engine before turning in his seat

to look at her. 'Very politely said, May,' he said dryly. 'But which part of the evening are you thanking me for—the meal, or the company? Because, to my knowledge, you didn't enjoy either one!' he added hardly.

'Nevertheless, thank you,' May insisted distantly before turning to open the door and get out of the car without a second glance.

But instead of going straight into the farmhouse she walked over to barn where the last of the newly delivered ewes and lambs were being kept for the moment, switching on the low light over the door as she went in. She had already noted the lights on in the farmhouse when they'd arrived, knew that her two sisters and their fiancés were probably still up, and unwilling for the moment to go inside and face them all. Especially as they would probably all be filled with curiosity concerning her evening out with Jude.

An evening that had been a disaster from start to finish, she readily acknowledged as she dropped down onto one of the bales of hay, burying her face in her hands in total despair.

What was she going to do?

What could she do, when, despite May's request for her not to do so, at any moment April Robine herself could come to the farm and reveal her identity to January and March? And if the other woman did that, what were January and March going to make of May's duplicity all these years?

'May…?'

She looked up defensively at the sound of Jude's voice in the semi-darkness, the first indication she had had that he'd followed her into the barn rather than driving straight off after she'd got out of the car.

'What do you want?' she demanded, hastily wiping the tears from her cheeks as he advanced into the barn.

Jude drew in a harsh breath. 'Why haven't you gone into the farmhouse?'

She gave a humourless smile. 'Why do you think?'

He moved forward, coming to sit beside her on the bale of hay. 'I meant what I said earlier. About it being time someone was there for you for a change,' he explained abruptly at her questioning look. 'I'll be there for you. If you'll let me.'

May gave him a quizzical look. Exactly what did he mean by that remark?

Whatever he meant, she knew she couldn't accept his offer, had to deal with this alone. As she had since her father had died.

'Maybe there is a way in which you can help me, Jude,' she said slowly.

He tilted his head to one side. 'Yes?'

She straightened determinedly. 'Buy the farm. Immediately.'

He sat back as if she had struck him. 'Buy the farm...? But—'

'Immediately,' she repeated as the idea began to grow and take shape in her mind. 'January and March can be married in London; both Will and Max are based there anyway. And—'

'And what about you?' Jude cut in harshly. 'What are you going to do? Accept David Melton's offer, after all?'

'Of course not,' she dismissed impatiently. 'That would defeat the whole object—'

'Because getting away from April, as quickly and as far as possible, is the object,' Jude finished disgustedly, turning to grasp the tops of May's arms. 'May, didn't you listen to anything I said to you earlier? Can't you see that my buying the farm under these conditions, with the sole intention of taking your sisters and yourself away from here, isn't going to solve a thing?' He shook her slightly. 'April is here now. She's real. And nothing you can do or say is going to change that.'

May shook her head determinedly. 'Once she realises that I meant what I said earlier, she'll go away again. Back to America—'

'And what did you say to her that would make her do that?' Jude frowned.

Her chin rose defiantly. 'The truth, that January and March believe she's dead—'

'I saw the look on April's face earlier today, May,' Jude cut in insistently. 'April is longing to see January and March. Wants, as she already has with you, to see the women they have become—'

'She has no right!' May cried agitatedly, standing up abruptly, uncaring as she hurt her arms wrenching out of Jude's grasp.

He grimaced. 'Obviously April believes she does. Look, May, I can't even begin to understand what happened here over twenty years ago, but—'

'She left us, walked out on the three of us when we were only babies; I, for one, don't need to know any more than that,' May assured him scathingly.

'She walked out on your father, too, May,' Jude said quietly.

'And it almost killed him,' she acknowledged harshly. 'I know, because I watched what her desertion did to him. He never married again, you know—'

'Neither has April,' he pointed out softly.

She shook her head. 'I'm not interested in what *she* has or hasn't done. Don't you see? This is all your fault, Jude,' she turned on him accusingly. 'None of this would have happened if you had never come here and brought her with you—' Her words were cut off abruptly as Jude stood up to pull her forcefully against him, his mouth coming fiercely down on hers.

It was a kiss that May, after the first few seconds of struggle, returned just as fiercely as emotions quickly spiralled out of control.

Here, now, nothing else mattered but the fiery passion that blazed so strongly between them, May returning kiss for kiss, caress for caress, her hands against the naked warmth of his chest as she shed first his jacket and then his shirt.

Jude's mouth was warm against the arched column of her neck, teeth gently biting her earlobes before his tongue moved moistly to the dark hollows that shadowed the base of her throat, discarding her jacket to pull the zip to her dress slowly down the length of her spine.

The hay was warm and soft beneath them as they lay down upon it, Jude half lying across her as his lips returned to possess hers.

May gasped her pleasure as Jude's hand moved to cup her breast, feeling his touch through the silky material of her bra, the nipple already pert and aroused, Jude's tongue searching the heated moisture of her mouth.

She wanted him, how she wanted him. All of him.

Her back arched instinctively as Jude's lips moved to the naked pertness of her breasts, paying homage to each as he kissed their arousal, tongue laving the rosy tips as pleasure rippled uncontrollably through every particle of May's being, his hand moving softly across the flat planes of her stomach to the lace panties beneath.

Her fingers convulsed fiercely in the darkness of his hair as she held him to her, wanting him never to stop, wanting this pleasure never to end.

Heat began in the centre of her body, deep inside her, rising quickly as it pervaded all of her body, on fire now as the hitherto unknown sensations caused her body to arch and then fall down, down, down…

'It's all right, May.' Jude suddenly cradled her fiercely into the hardness of his body. 'It's all right,' he soothed as the spasms continued to rack her fevered body.

Reality came back with the force of a blow as May realised exactly what had just happened between them, what she had allowed to happen.

It wasn't 'all right'.

How could it be, when she was so deeply in love with this man…?

Jude felt May moving emotionally and mentally away from him even as he continued to hold her physically close to him.

He hadn't meant for this to happen, hadn't intended—

Of course he hadn't intended for any of this to happen, but he could already feel the way May was putting her barriers back in place, even higher now that she knew he was capable of breaching them even beyond her imagining.

But it was beyond his own imagining, too. How could he ever have known? He had never thought…

May's response to him, his to her, was a complete revelation to him, too, completely beyond any other experience he had ever known. Even now, when he could feel her drawing away from him, he wanted her. And not just physically…

'Let me go, Jude,' she rasped coldly.

He drew in a ragged breath, making no move to comply. 'May—'

'I said let me go.' Her voice was like ice now, although she made no move to push him away from her, acquiescent but removed as she lay lifeless in his arms.

There was no need for her to push him away, Jude knowing her withdrawal from him was already complete, no matter how close in proximity they might still be physically.

And they were close, their near-naked bodies still entwined, Jude able to feel the slender length of her against him from shoulder to thigh, the dark silkiness of her hair against his face.

But in reality she might as well have been a million miles away.

And it shouldn't be like this. What they had just shared, their completely uninhibited response to each other, was something to explore further, not deny.

As May was denying it, even now sitting up to straighten her dress, her face deliberately turned away from his in the dim light given off by the low bulb overhead.

'May, I'm not going to leave this here,' he assured her determinedly even as he pulled on his shirt and buttoned it with slightly unsteady fingers.

'Leave what here, Jude?' She seemed to have recovered slightly, her voice scathing now. 'We've had a little romp in the hay, that's all—'

'No, it is not all, damn it!' he rasped furiously, eyes glittering with the emotion as he turned to look at her. 'Just now—what happened between us—' He drew in a deep breath, choosing his words carefully. 'That isn't usual, May.'

'Sexual desire isn't usual?' she returned mockingly, standing up to move away from him. 'You have straw in your hair,' she added derisively.

'So do you,' he dismissed impatiently, moving to stand beside her. 'May, that wasn't just sexual desire—'

'Of course it was,' she insisted waspishly. 'Admittedly, it went a little too far, but that's probably because emotions were running high anyway—'

'Stop it, May!' he rasped harshly, his hands once again grasping her arms as he held her immobile in front of him. 'I can't say I'm any happier about this revelation than you appear to be, but—'

'Revelation?' she repeated scathingly, green eyes hard as she looked up at him unflinchingly. 'As far as I'm concerned, the only revelation that took place here tonight was that I'm not as immune to physical attraction as I thought I was.' She gave a shrug. 'I'll know better another time,' she added hardly.

Jude looked down at her with narrowed eyes, his gaze searching on the shadows of her face, finding nothing but cold dismissal in her expression, green eyes deliberately unreadable.

His hands dropped away from her arms. 'That's all this was to you—physical attraction?'

'What else?' she scorned dryly. 'We seem to have been sending sparks off each other, in one way or another, since we first met. Tonight, what just happened, was just a natural outlet for those sparks.' She shook her head, her smile self-derisive. 'It was better than hitting each other, I suppose!'

Jude looked at her frustratedly now. Did she really believe what she was saying? Or was she just as disturbed by their reaction to each other as he was, but chose to belittle its importance rather than confront it? Because he couldn't believe, from what he knew of May, from what he had come to know of her whole family, that she had ever behaved in this abandoned way with any man before him.

Or was it just that he wanted to believe that she hadn't…?

Why the hell would he want to believe that?

He had been involved with quite a lot of women during his thirty-seven years, and he had never expected any of them to be untouched, a virgin, so why should he imagine that May was? Why should he want her to be?

Because he did.

That was the only answer he could give himself for the moment. The only answer he could accept for the moment. Because, loath as he was to admit it, he was more disturbed by his response to May, by her response to him, than she appeared to be.

He needed to get away from here—far away from May—to try and work out for himself exactly what all this meant.

His mouth thinned. 'Perhaps you should go inside now,' he rasped dismissively, bending down to retrieve his jacket, shaking the straw from it before putting it back on. 'No doubt your sisters have seen the car outside and are wondering what's happened to us both,' he added ruefully, having been completely aware of the interest shown earlier by Will, Max and the two younger Calendar sisters in the two of them spending the evening together. But, like May, he had chosen not to satisfy that curiosity. How much longer he would be able to continue doing that, he had no idea.

May nodded abruptly. 'I—would rather you didn't come in with me,' she told him huskily, her face now slightly pale in the semi-darkness.

He gave a humourless smile. 'I hadn't imagined that

I would,' he conceded dryly, that smile turning to a scowl as he lifted a hand and May instantly flinched away from him. 'I was only going to remove the straw from your hair,' he rasped harshly.

'Oh.' Colour heightened her cheeks now. 'Sorry,' she muttered, no longer meeting his gaze.

Jude frowned grimly as he concentrated on removing the straw from the darkness of her hair, his movements deliberately businesslike, all the time knowing that one movement of encouragement on May's part, even the slightest relenting in her stony expression, and he would sweep her back into his arms. And this time he wouldn't be able to let her go.

But it was as if she sensed that, stepping sharply away from him as soon as all of the hay had been removed from her hair, turning away from him as she picked up her own discarded jacket.

He couldn't let her go like this.

But what choice did he have? He still had no idea himself what was going on between himself and May. Only that something was. And it was a 'something' he didn't want in his life.

Which left them precisely where?

Nowhere, he realised heavily.

But he didn't want to be 'nowhere' with May, wanted— What did he want? Until he knew that, until he completely understood his own feelings of wanting her but at the same time needing to push her away from him, he had no choice but to let May go.

Even if that meant that her barriers against him would be so much higher the next time the two of them met?

Even then, he told himself firmly. Maybe it would even be better, for both of them, if her barriers were so high he didn't stand a chance of crossing them. Ever.

'I'll walk you back to your car,' she told him stiltedly as she walked towards the door.

His mouth twisted grimly. 'Making sure I've left the premises this time?'

May shrugged. 'I doubt anyone could make you do anything you didn't want to do!'

This woman could, Jude realised with shocking clarity. Even now he wanted to draw her back into his arms, to kiss her until they were both senseless.

Again…

'No, they couldn't,' he confirmed abruptly at the same time as he inwardly acknowledged his reluctance to go, to leave this woman.

Which was exactly the reason he had to go. Now!

'Would you tell Max that I'll call him tomorrow?' he said abruptly.

May nodded distantly. 'I'll tell him.'

'Thanks,' he accepted tersely before getting back inside the car to start the engine, raise a hand in brief farewell and drive away.

Don't look back, Jude, he told himself firmly. This woman meant trouble for him. With a capital T.

Don't look back!

His glance moved to the driving mirror as if drawn by a magnet, May still standing in the farmyard exactly where he had left her, moonlight showing her in stark relief, her face white against the darkness of her hair.

His Nemesis…?

All his adult life he had gone where he wanted, done what he wanted, enjoying brief, meaningless relationships with women if they happened to present themselves.

Now the thought of not being with May, the possibility of not seeing her again, had shattered into a million pieces all his carefully constructed life of no ties, no commitments.

The question was: what was he going to do about it? If anything…

CHAPTER TWELVE

'THAT was Jude,' Max informed May as he strolled back into the barn where she was placing eggs in trays.

'Oh?' May kept her voice deliberately light, at the same time as her heart began to beat more rapidly in her chest.

May had assumed, when March had called over to Max as he'd helped her with the egg-collecting that he had a telephone call, that it might be Jude; it was still too early in the day for anyone but a close friend to have rung.

It had been quite bemusing watching the fastidious Max as he'd moved around the far-from-clean henhouse collecting the eggs for her, after declaring that he had every intention of being a help rather than a nuisance while he was staying here.

But all thought of amusement had faded when March had called him into the farmhouse to take the telephone call, May wondering exactly what Jude was calling the other man about, as taut as wire by the time Max rejoined her.

She glanced up at him now, noting the slight frown between his eyes. 'Everything all right?' Once again she kept her tone deliberately light.

'Fine,' he confirmed ruefully. 'Jude has to go away for a few days, that's all,' he added dismissively.

Had to? Or had Jude simply decided to do so?

May's heart had skipped a beat at the news, although she wasn't sure whether it was from relief or despair.

After last night, half of her wished she never had to see Jude ever again, and the other half longed to do so. Because she loved him with all her being!

She curled up inside every time she thought of being in Jude's arms the previous evening, of the intimacies they had shared; how could they possibly face each other again without remembering that intimacy?

They couldn't, was the obvious answer, and maybe these few days' reprieve were exactly what she needed to face that moment if—when—it came. The fact that Jude had removed himself from the area pointed to the fact that he wasn't too eager for the confrontation, either!

But, unfortunately, it also meant there was no possibility of him taking up her offer of selling the farm to him immediately…

Which, the awkwardness with Jude apart, left her with the same problem as yesterday: how did she avoid April Robine coming here and introducing herself to January and March?

'Er—' she gave Max a bright, meaningless smile '—is Jude going away on his own, or is Miss Robine accompanying him?' If April were going, too, then that would solve that problem for a day or so, too.

Max gave her a searching look, May returning that look—she hoped—with smiling indifference.

May had come to know Max quite well over the last few weeks, knew he was a man of deep reserve, that aloofness no shield for his undoubted intelligence.

Although, January had confided in her yesterday, Max seemed to be making some effort to actually contact his own estranged mother, with a view to at least removing the strained relationship that had existed between them since his mother's desertion of her husband and son when Max was still only a child.

May hadn't known whether to laugh or cry yesterday when January had sat and told her all this as the two of them had enjoyed a cup of coffee together, the situation so like the one that May now found herself in with their own mother.

Although, for obvious reasons, she hadn't been able to tell January any of that...

'I didn't ask,' Max finally answered her. 'Is it important?' he added softly.

'Of course not,' May dismissed briskly—a little too brisk, she realised as Max gave a troubled frown. 'January wasn't breaking any confidences, but she mentioned to me yesterday that you are trying to contact your mother, that you may be inviting her to the wedding?' She deliberately made an abrupt change of subject.

Max's brow instantly cleared. 'I'm thinking of it,' he confirmed dryly. 'Meeting January, falling in love with her, being loved in return, has changed my outlook on things somewhat,' he acknowledged ruefully.

'I would think it might.' May smiled warmly.

He nodded. 'I've come to realise that not everything is as black and white as I always liked to think it was, that what happened over thirty years ago, seen through the eyes of a young child, didn't necessarily happen the way I remember it,' he added self-derisively.

May gave him a frustrated look; nothing Max had said so far, about his own mother's desertion, was helping with the situation she now found herself in with April. Was it really that easy? she wondered. Was it possible to forgive, if not forget, the childhood abandonment by one's parent?

'What is it, May?' Max prompted concernedly. 'You've been very—preoccupied, since we all came back,' he explained at her questioning look. 'Not your normal self at all.'

May gave him an inquisitive look. 'And just what is my "normal" self?' she said ruefully.

He shrugged. 'Calm. Decisive. Level-headed. Able to see a situation clearly where others sometimes can't,' he added, obviously referring to his own inability a few weeks ago to recognise his true feelings for January.

And, like Max, May knew she was no longer any of the things he had described her as being.

Because of Jude. Because of April Robine. Just because of this whole awful, complicated situation.

'Jude mentioned to me that you have offered to sell the farm to him, after all,' Max continued evenly.

May could feel the guilty colour heighten in her cheeks. Of course there was no reason why Jude shouldn't have mentioned the offer to Max; he was still the other man's lawyer, after all. It was just... 'Then he shouldn't have done,' she snapped. 'I haven't had chance to discuss it with January and March yet—'

'It doesn't matter.' Max shook his head dismissively. 'May, Jude isn't going to accept the offer.'

She became very still, her expression puzzled now. 'He isn't?'

'No,' Max confirmed wryly.

'Why isn't he?' she demanded frustratedly. 'It was what he wanted. What he came here for. What on earth—?'

'The reason he telephoned me just now was to ask me while he's away to submit Will's second set of plans, the ones excluding this farm, to the local planning committee,' Max informed her quietly.

May was well aware of the fact that Will, as Jude's architect, had drawn up two sets of plans for the proposed health and country club he intended building on the neighbouring Hanworth Estate, also knew that one of those sets of plans included this farm, and that the other one didn't. The question was, why was Jude choosing to submit the latter?

She shook her head. 'I don't understand.'

'Actually—' Max gave a rueful smile '—neither do I.'

May burst out laughing at this blunt admission from a man who, as a lawyer, was often carefully ambiguous in his own statements. 'Well, that's honest, I suppose,' she conceded. 'Although it doesn't help me, does it?' she added frowningly.

'Not if you're really serious about selling, no.' Max grimaced. 'You can be sure that January and March will agree to anything you decide to do about the farm,' he assured lightly. 'After all, it's you it affects the most.'

Yes, it was, and in the circumstances she had decided the best thing to do was sell. The problem with that appeared to be that Jude no longer wanted to buy.

She frowned darkly, quickly coming to a decision. 'Max, has Jude already gone? Or is he still at the hotel?'

Max looked momentarily stunned by the question, and then he gave a rueful shrug. 'I don't think he was calling from his mobile, so I presume he must still be at the hotel— May, where are you going?' he called as she spun on her heel and walked quickly towards the door of the shed where they had been working.

She glanced back at him briefly. 'To the hotel, of course.'

'But—'

'Max—' she turned back impatiently '—did Jude tell you when he would be coming back?'

'No,' Max answered slowly.

She nodded. 'Then there's no telling when that will be, is there? In which case, I intend talking to him before he leaves.' Jude might have time to waste, but she certainly didn't.

'Do you want me to come with you?' Max offered softly.

May became very still. She would like nothing better than the moral support, at least, of the company of this self-assured man who was in love with her youngest sister. But at the same time she appreciated that each time she and Jude had spoken together the last couple of days their conversation had always returned to the subject of her connection to April Robine—and that was something May did not intend discussing in front of Max.

She gave him a grateful smile. 'It's good of you to offer, but no, thanks. I'm sure I'll be fine on my own,' she assured with a lot more confidence than she actually felt.

Max didn't look in the least reassured by her words, either, frowning darkly. 'Are you sure? Jude sounded— a little terse, this morning,' he warned ruefully.

At the moment, sensitive as May was to her own love for him, a terse Jude Marshall would be preferable to the seductive one of last night. 'I'm sure.' She nodded confidently. 'If you wouldn't mind continuing to collect the eggs for me…?' she added teasingly.

'Not at all.' Max returned her smile. 'This last couple of days have been a complete leveller for me; I had no idea how hard farmers have to work.' He grimaced.

May gave an appreciative laugh as she let herself out of the shed, although her smile faded to a look of grim determination as she made her way quickly to her car.

If she gave herself too much time to think then the mountain might just change its mind about going to Mohammed!

Jude came to an abrupt halt as he stepped out of the lift, completely unprepared for the sight of May, having spotted him alighting from the lift, striding confidently towards him across the reception area of the hotel.

Despite the earliness of the hour, several other heads turned to look in her direction as she walked towards him, including that of the wide-eyed receptionist. Not surprising, really—May looked as if she had come here straight from the farmyard, her coat old and mud-stained, with disreputable jeans tucked into muddy wellington boots, and the latter were making a terrible mess of the pristine whiteness of the hotel floor tiles.

The situation might have been funny at any other time, but, still raw from their encounter the previous evening, Jude wasn't in the least pleased to see May here, muddy boots or not.

He hadn't slept at all the previous night, had paced the hotel suite for hours as he'd tried to come to some sort of inner acceptance of what had happened between himself and May, to clarify and then dismiss it as just a situation that had got completely out of hand. He had tried to do that...

By the time daylight had appeared through the windows Jude had known he was no further towards doing that than he had been the previous evening, deciding that he had to follow his initial reaction—and that was to get himself away from May, from this situation, and hope that he would be able to make sense of it then.

Seeing May again before he left had not been part of his plans.

He scowled down at her as she came to an abrupt halt

in front of him, eyes deeply green against the whiteness of her face. Eyes the same deep green as April's...

His mouth tightened as he remembered May's complete implacability over that situation. 'What do you want?' he rasped unwelcomingly, gaze narrowing ominously as she seemed to flinch at his words. 'You're making a hell of a mess of the floor,' he added disgustedly.

May blinked, instantly looking down, eyes widening self-consciously as she seemed to realise for the first time that she was wearing muddy boots. 'Never mind.' Her chin rose challengingly as she looked back at him. 'I'm sure they'll add the cost of cleaning it to your bill.'

Despite himself, Jude felt his mouth twitch with amusement; not too much bothered this woman, did it? 'I'm sure they will,' he acknowledged dryly. 'So, what can I do for you, May?' he prompted wearily.

'Max told me you've asked him to submit the final architect plans that don't include the farm,' she told him bluntly.

Jude drew in a sharp breath. Damn Max for doing that. Jude had thought he would be long gone by the time May discovered what he had done. But at least now he knew the reason that May had turned up here so suddenly...

Not that he had thought for one moment that it was a change of heart on her part—

Hadn't he?

Hadn't some part of him begun to hope that perhaps she felt more towards him than physical attraction? And even if she did, what then? Jude deliberately shied away from that thought. She hadn't realised anything like that. Her only interest in him was still the farm.

His mouth thinned. 'Then he had no right to tell you—'

'You told him first of my offer to sell the farm,' May defended heatedly.

They could go on like this all morning, Jude realised heavily; to his knowledge, May had never backed down from an argument yet.

'So?' He was deliberately obstructive; this woman had caused him nothing but grief since he had first met her, and his previous night of no sleep hadn't helped his mood one little bit.

Her cheeks flushed angrily. 'So I had told you I would sell it to you,' she reminded tautly.

'Immediately.' He nodded uninterestedly.

'Well?' May demanded impatiently.

'I seem to remember that I told you I am no longer interested in buying it,' Jude replied calmly.

Her eyes sparked deeply green. 'You're just being bloody-minded now.'

He raised dark brows. 'I am?'

'Yes, you are,' she snapped. 'I don't—'

'May, could we go and sit down somewhere?' he interrupted dryly. 'We're attracting a certain amount of attention standing here,' he explained as she frowned her irritation with the suggestion. Not that it particularly bothered him who was watching them, but he had a feeling, with hindsight, that May just might.

She glanced around them impatiently, affording the receptionist a less than friendly scowl as the other woman ogled them unashamedly, obviously fascinated by the stark contrast they made, Jude dressed in a business suit, shirt and tie, May looking more like a tramp who had walked in off the street in the hope of being given a warming cup of coffee by some charitable guest.

May turned back to him impatiently. 'I really don't give a damn what they think—'

'But I do.' Jude clasped her arm, turning her firmly in the direction of the deserted lounge just to the left of where they stood. 'Sit,' he instructed as she made no effort to do so.

'I'll make the seats all dirty, too,' she answered dismissively. 'Jude, you're just being difficult because I—'

'No doubt they will put that on my bill, too,' he rasped. 'I said sit, May,' he bit out through gritted teeth as she stood facing him. 'And think very carefully before you continue that previous statement,' he added grimly as she sank reluctantly into one of the armchairs.

'Because I refuse to listen to you concerning April…' she finished with obvious puzzlement for his grim attitude.

Ah, April…

Jude gave an inner wince for the mistake he had almost made. Of course May hadn't been going to refer to her dismissal last night of the intimacies they had shared…

'I think you're being unreasonable about that, yes.' He nodded confirmation as he sat down opposite her. 'But it in no way affects my decision concerning the farm,' he added hardly as she would have spoken. 'I don't work that way, May.'

'No?' she came back challengingly. 'It seems to me that you do.' She didn't wait for him to answer. 'Your sole purpose in coming here was to purchase the farm, and now that it's been offered to you you say you don't want it!' She shook her head. 'That doesn't make any sense to me. Unless—'

'I said I don't work that way, May,' he bit out grimly.

'But you wanted the farm so badly a month ago,' she reminded exasperatedly.

So badly he had sent Max here for the sole purpose of purchasing it, no matter what the cost. And instead of acquiring the farm for him Max had ended up falling in love with the youngest Calendar sister. And then Will had arrived to draw up the plans for the proposed health and country club, only to fall in love with the middle Calendar sister. And so he had finally come here himself to see what on earth was going on. Only to—

'And now I don't,' he rasped, knowing that in future he wanted as little to do with May Calendar as possible. 'Look, May—what the hell—?' Jude broke off his involuntary exclamation to stare dazedly across the reception area.

As if his thinking of them had conjured them into being, he could now see Max and Will, January and March entering the hotel, all of them looking as disreputable as May in the clothes they had obviously been wearing this morning to work on the farm.

'Is this some sort of delegation?' Jude turned to challenge May impatiently even as he stood up slowly.

But one look at May's face, the colour slowly draining from it, was enough to show him that the arrival at the hotel of her two sisters, at least, was the very last thing she wanted.

And Jude knew exactly why that was…

CHAPTER THIRTEEN

WHAT on earth were they *doing* here?

The next question, following on quickly from the first, was what was she going to do? April Robine was still somewhere in this hotel, could come into the reception area at any moment...

May turned frantically to Jude, appreciating that after last night he was probably the last person she could ask for help, but also knowing that perhaps he was also the only one who could help her at this moment.

'Do something,' she hissed breathlessly, the other four not having spotted them sitting in the lounge yet, talking to the receptionist at this moment, probably asking her where Jude could be found.

Jude looked down at her, dark brows raised. 'Like what?'

'I don't know,' May returned exasperatedly. 'They're your friends; get rid of them.'

He shrugged. 'They're your sisters, and their fiancés, you get rid of them.'

'Thanks for nothing!' May snapped disgustedly, feeling her panic rise as, having been told exactly where Jude could be located, four pairs of eyes now turned in their direction. 'Jude...!' she pleaded, desperately clutching his arm now.

He looked down at her frowningly for several long seconds before his gaze shifted to her hand tightly grasping his arm. 'Okay,' he agreed briskly, seeming to have come to some sort of decision. 'But whatever I say, back me up, hmm?'

Now it was May's turn to frown; she didn't like the sound of this one little bit.

But what choice did she have but to trust him? None, came the resounding answer.

'Fine,' she acknowledged hastily before turning smilingly to greet her sisters, Max and Will. 'What are you all doing here?' she prompted lightly, receiving a slightly apologetic grimace from Max, who had obviously been badgered into telling her sisters where she had gone.

'Looking for you,' the outspoken March answered bluntly. 'What are you doing here?' Her eyes were narrowed with suspicion.

May drew in a deep breath, wondering when Jude was going to start saying something. 'I—'

'She was getting herself engaged to me,' Jude announced lightly.

May's head snapped up as she stared at him in total astonishment. He called that saying something. Well, it was certainly that, but how on earth was she supposed to back him up in a claim like that…?

It didn't help that he now looked slightly dazed at his own comment, as if unaware himself of what he had been going to say until after he had said it…

'Congratulations!' Will was the first of the four newcomers to find his voice, moving forward to kiss May lightly on the cheek before shaking Jude warmly by the hand. 'Looks like the Calendar charm worked its magic again,' he added with a grin.

May was still staring at Jude, totally transfixed. Why on earth had he said something so stupid? Worse, how did he think they were ever going to be able to extricate themselves from such an announcement?

More to the point, what good had announcing their engagement done towards encouraging her sisters and their fiancés to leave the hotel?

'Welcome to the family, Jude.' January moved on tiptoe to kiss him lightly on the cheek before turning to hug May.

'Welcome, Jude.' March nodded, a little more reserved in her congratulations towards him, although she gave May a rib-crushing hug seconds later.

Only Max, it seemed, with his added astuteness from his conversation with May earlier this morning, sensed that something wasn't quite right about this situation, his brows raised questioningly at May over March's shoulder.

She gave a barely perceptible shake of her head; she had no idea what was going on, so how could she possibly even begin to explain it to Max?

Jude, the instigator of this situation, still seemed totally nonplussed by his own behaviour, although the dazed look was starting to leave his face now as his expression became more unreadable by the second.

'It's a little early, but I think champagne is in order, don't you?' Will announced happily.

May glared at Jude, still willing him to say something, do something, to get them all to leave. Although, going on his last effort, perhaps he had better not bother.

She turned back to the others. 'We're hardly dressed for it, are we?' she dismissed lightly with a pointed grimace at their disreputable clothing; Jude was the only smartly dressed one amongst them. 'I thought we would all go back to the farm—'

'And break up the party?' Jude smiled, finally seemed

to have found his voice, moving closer to May now as his arm moved lightly about her waist. 'Champagne sounds like a wonderful idea.'

'I'll go and ask the receptionist to bring us some.' Max spoke quietly. 'Would you like to come with me, May?' he prompted softly.

May gave him a grateful smile; even a few moments' respite from what was turning into a complete farce would be welcome.

'It doesn't take two of you to order champagne, Max,' Jude was the one to answer him before May even had a chance to do so, his arm tightening about her waist. 'Besides, the road to love has been rather a rocky one, and I'm loath to have May away from me for even a few seconds,' he added huskily. 'She may just change her mind between here and the reception desk,' he added with a challenging look in her direction.

Change her mind! Making her mind up in the first place would have been rather nice.

Not that she thought for a moment that this engagement was meant to be a real one. She wouldn't be feeling so desperately unhappy if it were.

She had known after last night how deeply in love she was with Jude. Completely. Utterly. There was no way she would have responded to him in the way she had if she weren't. Which was why his announcement just now, made for appearances' sake only, gave her such an aching pain in the region of her heart...

'May and I will go and order the champagne,' Jude assured the other man. 'You all make yourselves comfortable. We won't be long.'

Long enough, May hoped, for her to tell him exactly what she thought of his effort to help the situation—it was now ten times worse.

*   *   *

'Wait,' Jude instructed as May turned to him as soon as they had left the lounge.

'You—'

'I *said* wait, May,' he repeated tautly, having been expecting this verbal reprimand as soon as they were alone, but nevertheless choosing to delay it for a few more minutes. 'In fact, wait here while I order the champagne.' He grasped her shoulders to halt her several feet short of the reception desk, walking on alone.

Not that he didn't think May had a perfect right to be furious with him for having announced their engagement in that unexpected way; he had been more than a little stunned by it himself.

But having once made the announcement, he had begun to realise that he actually liked the sound of it, that the thought of being engaged to May wasn't an unpleasant prospect at all. In fact, the more the idea sank in, he realised it was exactly what he wanted.

He had been fighting his feelings for her for days now, choosing to put many different labels on his behaviour rather than face up to the real reason he felt so protective towards her. He had even thought, by leaving this morning, that once May was out of sight she would also be out of mind. What an idiot!

He was in love with May Calendar...

The thought of not seeing her, not being with her, even not arguing with her, was a completely unpalatable one.

If she hadn't arrived at the hotel in the way that she had, how far would he have got? To the motorway? All the way to London? Or would he have got as far as the borders of Yorkshire and realised that in leaving May he had left the most important part of himself behind?

The latter, he now believed…

But he hadn't known, really hadn't realised—or just refused to accept…?—the way he felt about her, until he'd heard himself announce their engagement. And then it had all become amazingly clear, so utterly right that he knew he was fighting a losing battle in trying to leave her. Separation wouldn't change the way he felt about her, it would only make that separation harder to bear.

How to convince May of that—that was the question.

How ironic. The self-assured, self-contained Jude Marshall, brought to his emotional knees for love of a woman who claimed to feel nothing but physical attraction towards him. It would be funny if it weren't so heart-wrenchingly painful.

'Champagne's on its way,' he told her lightly as he returned to her side. 'Cheer up, May,' he added mockingly, not at all reassured by the paleness of her face. 'It's only an engagement, not an actual wedding.' Persuading May into marrying him was going to be much more difficult.

She shook her head. 'It isn't that,' she breathed huskily, looking past him now, her eyes having taken on a haunted look. 'April Robine just came down in the lift…!' she added weakly.

Jude turned sharply, just in time to see April stepping out of the lift, turning to laugh huskily at the person who accompanied her.

Jude's eyes widened as he saw David Melton follow April into the reception area, knowing by the way that May stiffened at his side that she had also seen the other man, added two and two together, with the earliness of the hour, and probably come up with the same conclusion that Jude had—David Melton had spent the night at the hotel.

Great. In all the time Jude had been friends with April, which was getting on for six months now, he had never known her to be involved with anyone, romantically or otherwise. And now, when May already had such prejudice against her, April was obviously involved with the film director.

A man Jude still wasn't a hundred per cent certain that May didn't have feelings for herself...

Jude turned back to her decisively. 'It may not be what it looks, May,' he attempted to reassure her, at once struck by the irony of his protective feelings towards May actually stretching to the point where he didn't want anyone to hurt her, including another man.

A month ago, a week ago, he wouldn't have cared one way or the other about anyone else's actions, would have considered it their own business and no one else's, but with his newly realised feelings for May he knew that anyone, anyone at all, attempting to hurt her would bring his wrath down upon their head.

Her mouth twisted derisively, a pained look in her eyes. 'Of course it's what it appears,' she snapped dismissively. 'So tell me, Jude—' she looked up at him challengingly '—what do we do now?'

Good question.

But as he had no idea in which direction he was coming from—to keep April away from the two daughters who had lived in ignorance of her existence for over twenty years, or to punch David Melton on the nose for trifling with May's affections while so obviously involved with April, a move definitely guaranteed to draw attention to the other couple—Jude really had no idea.

Which was probably another first for him, he acknowledged.

No wonder he had chosen never to fall in love before; at the moment he didn't know whether he was on his head or his heels, and as for any feelings of positive action...

Chosen to fall in love.

Who was he kidding? There had been no choice involved in loving May; he simply did.

He gave a rueful grimace. 'We could always invite the two of them to join us for a glass of champagne?'

May glared up at him. 'Very funny. Now come up with an answer I would find acceptable.'

He didn't have one. He really didn't. But very soon the situation was going to be taken out of his hands anyway, April and David moving away from the lift now, which meant that at any moment they were going to see May and Jude standing a short distance away.

And then all hell was going to break loose.

CHAPTER FOURTEEN

MAY didn't have time to wonder what April was doing in the company of David Melton this early in the morning; the fact that April was standing only feet away was what held her immobile.

January and March were sitting in the lounge just across the reception area, and at any moment April might turn that beautiful head and see them there. There was absolutely no chance, once she had seen them, that the actress wouldn't recognise January and March for exactly who they were; the likeness between the three sisters was as unmistakable as their likeness to April herself.

She looked at April and David, turning slightly to look at her two sisters chatting away happily in the lounge, before turning back to April and David.

May couldn't breathe. Her head felt light! She was going to—

'You can't faint here,' Jude told her firmly as he took a grip of her arm.

Why couldn't she? If she were to faint, then—

'It's too late for that, anyway,' Jude murmured at her side.

It was too late, but it was David Melton who had spotted them rather than April, the film director leaning towards the beautiful actress to murmur something in her ear, April turning slowly towards them, her eyes deeply green in a face gone suddenly white.

And she hadn't even seen January and March yet.

May groaned inwardly, knowing the reason for the older woman's obvious distress was the memory of the last meeting between the two of them.

But what else could she have done but tell April to stay away from them, and in such a way that the other woman would have no doubts about how strongly May felt?

'I told you I would be here for you, May,' Jude reminded huskily, his grip tightening on her arm as the other couple began to walk in their direction.

Yes, he had told her that. But not that it would be as her so-called fiancé.

Could this situation get any worse than it was? May wondered dazedly.

'How fortuitous that we should see the two of you this morning,' David was the one to greet brightly. 'Just in time to celebrate the engagement.'

May turned to glare accusingly at Jude; she had thought his announcement just now had been completely spontaneous—the surprised look on his own face had seemed to imply that it was—but if the other couple were aware of it, too…

'David…' April murmured protestingly, the colour coming back into her cheeks as she gave May an embarrassed glance. 'I thought we were going to keep that to ourselves for a while?' she added awkwardly.

May looked from April to David, frowning as it dawned on her that David hadn't been referring to her own supposed engagement to Jude at all, but to his own. To April…

'We were,' David acknowledged apologetically, reaching out to squeeze April's hand reassuringly. 'But I thought, as May and Jude are actually here now…' He turned to raise questioning brows at May.

He knew. The knowledge was there, in his eyes, a mixture of compassion for her, and pleading on behalf of the woman he had just asked to marry him.

May's gaze shifted abruptly to April, easily able to read the uncertainty in her expression as she returned May's gaze, that same pleading in those deep green eyes.

What did they want from her? Pleasure? Forgiveness? Heartfelt congratulations? What?

Jude gave her arm a brief squeeze before stepping forward to kiss April lightly on one cheek. 'I'm very happy for you,' he told her huskily. 'David.' He held his hand out to the other man.

'Thanks.' David gave a boyish grin as he took the proffered hand.

Which left them all waiting for May's response…

She blinked, looking across at the woman who had been her mother, for the first time wondering—

Max had told her that not everything was as black and white as when seen through a child's eyes, that he had made mistakes about his own mother's actions; could there possibly, just possibly, be a way for her to be wrong about April, too? After all, as Jude had already pointed out to her, despite the fact that April was a beautiful and desirable woman, she hadn't remarried while their father was still alive…

May didn't know any more, had no idea how any of them were going to wipe out the past, all she did know was that she could no longer even try to control what was going to happen in the next few minutes.

'Congratulations, David,' she said warmly before turning to April. 'I'm very pleased for you, April,' she told the older woman huskily, moving forward to kiss her lightly on the cheek.

There were tears in April's eyes as she looked at her. 'Thank you,' she returned gratefully.

May looked at her wordlessly for several moments, her own vision blurring slightly as she felt close to tears herself.

This wouldn't do, she told herself firmly; the two of them couldn't just stand here blubbing.

She breathed deeply, knowing the moment of truth had arrived—whether she was ready for it or not. 'April, there are some people over here I would like you to meet,' she said evenly, moving to link her arm with April's as she turned her in the direction of the hotel lounge.

She heard April draw in a sharp breath beside her, turning to see April staring across to where March and January were sitting with Max and Will, also knowing that there could be no mistaking exactly who the two young women were.

'May...?' April choked at her side.

May gave an encouraging squeeze of her arm. 'It will be all right,' she told the other woman with more confidence than she actually felt; she really had no idea what was going to happen when April was introduced to March and January.

Did either of her sisters still remember their mother? Would they recognise the beautiful April Robine as being that woman?

None of them had ever discussed their mother as they were growing up, May because of the necessity of not distressing their father, her sisters just hadn't mentioned her after the first few months of asking where she had gone.

In truth, May really had no idea whether either of them would make the connection between the internationally acclaimed actress, April Robine, and the woman who had been their mother.

April swallowed hard, still staring across into the lounge, her voice huskily emotional when she spoke. 'They're both so beautiful. You all are,' she added shakily.

May gave a rueful smile. 'We all look like you.'

'They're all as kind and charming as you, too,' Jude cut in softly.

May turned to give him teasing smile. 'I'm not sure you've always thought that in my case.'

He gave an unapologetic shrug. 'I don't mind admitting when I'm wrong.'

Meaning that perhaps she shouldn't, either?

If she *was* wrong…

'Ah, the champagne has arrived,' Jude said with satisfaction as he saw the waitress crossing Reception with the laden tray, glad of something mundane to relieve the tension that was slowly building, his pride in May at that moment making him feel choked with emotion himself. 'I'm afraid we'll need two more glasses, and probably another bottle of champagne,' he told the middle-aged woman smilingly.

'Champagne?' David Melton raised puzzled blond brows as they began to follow the waitress into the lounge.

'We'll explain later,' Jude told the other man dismissively. 'Let's go and drink a toast to your and April's future happiness,' he encouraged briskly, his narrowed gaze fixed on May as she walked ahead of him beside April.

This couldn't be easy for her, he knew, and he wished there were something he could do to help her, at the same time knowing that all he could do was to be there for her, as he had promised he would. The question of their own engagement would, no doubt, come under discussion later.

When he would do everything within his power to persuade May into making it fact...

'Is it going to be all right, do you think?' David prompted frowningly at his side, his worried gaze also concentrated on April and May.

All right for whom? For April and her three daughters? Jude had no idea how January and March were going to react to meeting April, or if they were going to react at all. As for May, he still wasn't sure she didn't have feelings for this man at his side, and if she did, then her mother's engagement to David certainly wasn't going to help any possible future relationship she might have with April.

'We'll have to wait and see, won't we?' he returned unhelpfully, his newly found charitable feelings, because of his love for May, certainly not extending as far as the man at his side.

The four seated around the table stood up as they all entered the lounge, Jude quickly taking in their individual reactions to April's presence. Will looked admiring, as most men did when they first met April. Max looked pleased to renew their acquaintance. January and March were a little harder to read; after an initial brief glance at each other, their equally guarded gazes turned to May.

A May who was completely flustered as she tried to make the introductions.

'See to the champagne, hmm,' Jude instructed David Melton abruptly before stepping smoothly forward to stand at May's side, taking her hand into his to squeeze reassuringly. 'April and Max already know each other,' he lightly took over when May gave his hand a grateful squeeze back. 'Will Davenport,' he told April as she shook the other man's hand. 'My architect, on occasion, and also March's fiancé. And these two lovely ladies are May's sisters, March and January.' He smiled at the two of them.

His heart ached for April as she hesitated about what to do next, whether to shake the two sisters' hands, or just smile warmly. But as her hands were obviously shaking badly, and the smile was more than a little rocky, too, as she looked on the verge of tears, Jude had a feeling that April wasn't going to be able to achieve either with any degree of aplomb.

'And this is April's fiancé, David Melton.' May was the one to step into the breach as the film director began to hand around the full champagne glasses.

January took the glass he held out to her. 'Aren't you the film director who offered May a role in your film?' She frowned at him quizzically.

'I am,' he confirmed with a smile.

'April is to play the starring role in the film.' Once again it was May who spoke. 'David asked me to play the role of Stella, her daughter,' she added huskily.

Complete silence met this announcement, but Jude, deliberately watching March's and January's reactions this time, once again saw that look pass between the two younger sisters.

What did it mean?

Because there was definitely something in that look, something he couldn't read, but which the two sisters obviously could.

May was looking at her sisters anxiously now, obviously wondering if she had gone too far, her hand trembling slightly in his.

'Typecast, hmm.' The more outspoken March was the one to finally speak, grey-green hazel eyes gleaming with rueful laughter.

'What—?'

'You—'

Both May and April began to speak at once, both stopping abruptly to turn and look at each other before turning sharply back to look at January as she spoke.

'We know April is our mother, May,' she said reassuringly. 'We've always known,' she added with a shy glance in April's direction.

'Well, since we were old enough to watch one of your films on the television or go to the cinema,' March put in dryly.

Jude wasn't sure whether it was May or April who looked the more stunned by this last statement.

CHAPTER FIFTEEN

'I SIMPLY can't believe that the two of you have always known the truth.' May looked at March and January exasperatedly.

The eight of them had adjourned to the impartiality of Jude's hotel suite after the bluntness of January and March's admission, the four men having gravitated to the other end of this vast sitting-room, chatting away quite amiably as they sat and enjoyed the champagne, at the same time leaving the four women to the privacy they so desperately needed—even from the menfolk in their lives.

Although May wasn't too sure about the so-called 'man in her life', had no idea what she and Jude were going to do about their 'engagement' when all of this was over...

March gave a shrug. 'You and Dad always seemed so sensitive about the subject, so we just never mentioned it.' She turned to April. 'But we both knew the first time we saw one of your films. You don't forget your own mother,' she added huskily.

'Certainly not,' January confirmed forcefully. 'We've been so quietly proud of you,' she told April shyly.

May had to blink back the tears—again—at this further admission of her sisters' pact of silence concerning their mother, and she could see that April was visibly moved, too. Don't hurt them again, she silently willed the other woman. Please!

April swallowed hard, her face pale. 'I—'

'A little angry, too, of course,' March put in sharply. 'After all, we may have been proud of you, but we would much rather have had you at home. With us,' she added gruffly, her usually abrupt manner shaken for a moment.

April closed her eyes briefly, the tears escaping down the paleness of her cheeks, clinging to her lashes as she looked at them all once again. 'Believe it or not, I would much rather have been at home with you all, too—'

'But—'

'With you *all*,' April repeated firmly over the top of May's protest, holding her gaze steadily as she continued to speak. 'I loved the three of you, but I loved your father very much, too.'

Now May was completely thrown, had never thought— But Jude had pointed out to her only last night that April had never remarried; maybe she had never done so because she still loved their father…?

April gave a heavy sigh. 'I can see I shall have to try and explain it all to you—except I don't really understand it all myself.' Her hands twisted together in her lap. 'I was eighteen when I married your father, nineteen when May was born, and March and January obviously came along shortly after that, too,' she added affectionately. 'We were such a happy family.' She frowned. 'Everything was perfect. And then—I belonged to the local amateur dramatic society, was spotted by an agent, and offered a role in a play then touring the country, but ultimately arriving in London for a six-week run.'

So like her with the film role David had offered, May realised, also acknowledging the lure she had felt to accept the offer despite the upheaval it would have created on the farm. Had her mother felt that same pull, despite having a husband and children?

April grimaced. 'James wasn't happy about the situation, naturally. And for weeks I accepted that, knew that it wasn't really practical, that I had responsibilities.'

As May had realised she had responsibilities to March and January...

But she had acted on those responsibilities—their mother so obviously hadn't.

She gave Jude a less than confident smile as he looked across at her with frowning concern; it was still too early in this conversation to know where it was going exactly...

'I so wanted to do it, you see,' April acknowledged huskily. 'I was only twenty-four, and the chance to act, to go to London—it was like a fairy tale come true.' She gave a sigh. 'So I spoke to James about it again, explained that I could travel home on Sundays, that we could get someone in to look after you all with the money I would earn, that it would only be for a matter of weeks, that once I had done this thing it would be out of my system.'

May knew the aching need April was talking about, had felt it herself these last few weeks, a mixture of excitement at the prospect of succeeding, with disappointment that, because of the circumstances, she would never know the answer to that.

April shrugged. 'I pleaded with James to just let me have this one chance. He—he gave me an ultimatum, said that if I went out the door with the idea of acting in the play, that I would never come back in it.' She gave a shake of her head, her face white now. 'I didn't think he meant it.'

'But he did,' March said heavily.

April swallowed hard. 'Yes, he did. I couldn't believe it at first.' She shook her head. 'The company had toured as far as Manchester when I received a letter from a solicitor, accusing me of unreasonable behaviour for deserting my husband, and three children all under the age of five. I telephoned James immediately, of course, but he refused to speak to me, said that any communications between the two of us in future would be made through his lawyer.'

This was all news to May, but, despite her own anger towards April and her deep love for her father, she could actually believe that he was capable of doing what April said he had; May's love for him hadn't made her blind to the fact that James Calendar had been a hard, uncompromising man.

April's hands were gripped together so tightly now that her knuckles showed white. 'Your father received full custody of the three of you at the divorce, by claiming I was an unfit mother who had deserted her children in favour of an acting career, bringing in the fact that I was now of no particular fixed abode, with a career that was at best nefarious. I was given limited access, to be agreed with your father.' The tears began to fall again. 'He never agreed. We went back to court several times, but your father always had so many reasons why it wasn't practical for me to have the three of you to even stay with me, one of you had a cold and he wouldn't allow the other two to come without you, or the four of you had something else planned for the day I suggested. None of it was helped by the fact that I couldn't find any more work after the play had finished its run, that I was having to stay in a run-down boarding house. By the time I was in a position to have you with me, three years had passed. James assured me that none of you even remembered me,' she added achingly.

Oh, they had remembered their mother all right. All of them had, May now realised dazedly.

Max was right, nothing was ever completely black or white; there were always several shades of grey in between...

'I never stopped loving James,' their mother told them huskily. 'A part of me always continued to hope—but it wasn't to be.' She sighed softly. 'The whole situation went too far. There was no common ground on which we could agree, let alone come to terms over, least of all our children.' She grimaced. 'So I left England. Went to America to start again. And the rest, as they say, is history.' She looked down at her hands.

'Not quite.' May spoke up at last, more moved than she would ever have believed possible by what she had just heard. She wasn't sure she would have survived as composed and charming as April undoubtedly was if she had found herself in the same position. 'You didn't just move to America and forget about all of us—'

'Of course not.' April looked deeply shocked at the suggestion. 'Never a day went by when I didn't think about you, wonder what you looked like now, long to be there to share in your laughter, to dry your tears whenever you were hurt or upset. But it was all too difficult, because of the situation between your father and me, and so I—'

'You sent him money to help bring us up,' May put in softly, nodding confirmation of this fact to January and March as they gave her a surprised look; they didn't remember any luxurious influxes of money during their childhood, either. 'Dad never touched a penny of it,' she told them. 'I discovered it all sitting in a bank account after he died.'

'But—'

'How could he—?'

'Please don't blame your father,' April cut in on January's and March's protests. 'He—he did what he thought was for the best.'

May looked at her. 'You can still say that, after what he did to you, as well as to us?'

'I told you, I loved him. Always,' April added emotionally. 'I didn't know he had died until after—after the funeral, must have cried for a week once I learnt of his death. You don't have to be with someone in order to continue loving them,' she added simply.

'But afterwards.' March frowned. 'Why didn't you come to see us then?'

April gave the ghost of a smile. 'I thought I had.'

It all suddenly became crystal-clear to May; April's obvious friendship with David, his offer to her of a part in his film, the fact that April was to be the star of that film...

She looked at April with tear-wet eyes now. 'Did David know that it was your own daughter that you had asked him to come and watch act?'

April gave May a tearful smile at her astuteness. 'Not until I told him last night, no,' she acknowledged. 'He was as dumbfounded as everyone else has been!'

'But you *were* the one who sent him to Yorkshire to watch me in the pantomime, weren't you?' May realised emotionally.

It all made such sense now, David 'happening' to be in the audience that night, the fact that he had sought her out to offer the film role, his persistence since then, April's own appearance for added pressure.

'David's sister lives in the area—'

'I know that,' May dismissed impatiently. 'But it was

still you who asked him to come and watch me act, wasn't it?'

April gave her a concerned look. 'He wouldn't have offered you the part if he hadn't thought you were good enough—'

'I know that,' May assured her gently, her smile encouraging now. 'How did you know about my acting in the amateur dramatic society?'

April swallowed hard. 'I made a few enquiries about you all after your father died. I came to watch you one evening before talking to David. I—don't be cross, May,' she added pleadingly at May's start of surprise. 'Don't you understand, I had to finally see at least one of you?'

'Even if we didn't see you?' May frowned.

'Even then.' April nodded sadly.

May shook her head, standing up. 'I'm not in the least cross,' she assured huskily, moving to stand close to where April sat. 'I can't even begin to imagine what it must have been like for you all these years…!' she murmured emotionally. 'To know, and yet never to feel you had the right to—oh, Mum,' she choked tearfully as she bent down to hug the woman who was still her mother.

Jude had been watching the four women concernedly even while he gave the appearance of joining in the conversation with the other three men, an emotional lump in his throat as he saw May stand up and move forward to hug April, tears falling softly down the cheeks of both women.

It was going to be all right, he realised as January and March stood up to do the same thing, May standing to one side of them now, sobbing uncontrollably.

He stood up compulsively. 'If you gentlemen will ex-

cuse me?' he bit out abruptly, not even sparing them a
second glance as he crossed the room to May's side.
'Come with me,' he told her softly even as he took a
firm hold of her arm and took her through to the adjoin-
ing bedroom, closing the door firmly behind him before
taking her into his arms, gently stroking her hair as she
continued to cry against his shoulder.

'I'm so proud of you, May,' he told her gruffly. 'So
proud!'

He loved this woman—how he loved her—and seeing
her cry like this was like a physical pain.

'This is stupid,' May finally surfaced to murmur, wiping impatiently at her tear-wet cheeks. 'I have no idea
why I'm still crying,' she added disgustedly.

Jude moved to the bedside table and gave her a tissue
from the box there, giving her a few more seconds to
mop up the tears. The result, if she did but know it,
wasn't exactly flattering, her eyes puffy and bloodshot,
her cheeks blotched with red. But she still looked utterly
beautiful to Jude, so much so that he desperately wanted
to take her back in his arms and kiss her—something he
was sure she wouldn't welcome from him at the moment.

'It's been an emotional time for you all,' he murmured
noncommittally.

'Yes,' she acknowledged gruffly. 'I—we'll work it
out, Jude,' she assured him determinedly. 'Love, I've
just realised, makes people behave in strange ways.'

'Yes,' Jude confirmed flatly, thinking of his own reaction now to having fallen in love with May; he hadn't
exactly been gracious about it, had he?

Was it too late for them? Would May ever be able to

forgive him for some of the things he had said and done this last week? He certainly hoped so, because the thought of his life without her in it was a very bleak prospect, indeed…

CHAPTER SIXTEEN

MAY looked up at Jude, feeling almost shy with him now in the intimacy of his hotel bedroom. 'You were going away,' she reminded him.

'Yes,' he confirmed heavily. 'But I was coming back.' He indicated he obviously still had possession of the hotel suite, several of his personal belongings in the room, a couple of books on the bedside table, several suits hanging in the wardrobe.

'Oh.' She nodded, moistening dry lips. 'Are you still going?'

He drew in a ragged breath. 'Not if I can persuade you into making our engagement a reality, no...'

May looked up at him sharply, her gaze searching, looking for signs of mockery in his face. There weren't any, only the gleaming silver eyes showing any expression, and it wasn't mockery... 'Jude...?' she murmured uncertainly.

His hands clenched into fists at his sides. 'May, I've been a fool, an arrogant, pigheaded—' He broke off as she began to laugh. 'It isn't funny,' he said exasperatedly. 'Here I am trying to apologize, and you're laughing at me!'

'I'm not laughing at you, Jude.' She shook her head, her laughter stopping as quickly as it had started. 'I'm laughing at this whole stupid, painful situation.' She drew in a determined breath. 'Jude, I love you. Do you love me?' That breath lodged in her throat as she waited for his answer; if she had misunderstood what he had said a few minutes ago about their 'engagement' she was going to feel so stupid—

'How could I not love you?' Jude groaned emotionally. 'You're good, and kind, and honest—'

'Too much so on occasion,' she put in, a warm glow starting to build inside her, a warmth that was becoming stronger by the minute.

'Never that.' Jude gave a firm shake of his head. 'You're beautiful, desirable, everything that I could ever want in the woman I love—'

'You're making me blush now,' she murmured self-consciously as the warmth reached her cheeks. 'Jude...' She took a tentative step forward, still looking up at him uncertainly.

His hands moved up to cup either side of her face, his gaze intent on hers. 'Do you care for David Melton?'

'David...?' she echoed frowningly. 'Certainly not. What on earth—?'

'I love you, May Calendar,' Jude told her fiercely. 'I love you, I want to marry you and spend the rest of my life loving you. Will you have me?' he added less certainly.

Would she have him? The thought of Jude walking out of her life had been tearing her apart for days. Would she have him!

'Oh, yes,' she told him forcefully. 'But on one condition...' She held back slightly.

'Anything,' he promised without hesitation.

He really did love her. Not that May had had any doubts after what he had just said, but this complete capitulation confirmed it; there would be no half measures in their marriage. Ever.

'Buy the farm,' she told him huskily.

'But—'

'We all grew up there, and, despite everything, it was a happy childhood,' May continued determinedly. 'But it's time for us all to move on now. I will always love my father,' she told him huskily. 'But I think the future belongs to my mother.' Getting to know her, having her get to know all of them; it could take the rest of their lives. But, however long it took, May now accepted that April deserved to know her daughters.

'And us,' Jude prompted softly.

'Oh, definitely to us,' May assured him, her eyes glowing with her own love for him as she looked up at him confidently. 'I love you so much, Jude. So very much…!'

'You said it was only physical attraction,' he reminded her painfully.

'Self-protection,' she admitted huskily.

The next few minutes were taken up with Jude kissing her, thoroughly, purposefully, *deliciously*.

'We could make it a triple wedding,' he suggested some time later.

'So we could,' she immediately agreed. 'With April as the maid of honour, and David as best man—now that the original chief bridesmaid and best man have decided to get married themselves.'

It really was a wedding with a difference, Jude thought wryly as he stood at the church altar waiting for May to arrive at the church, Max and Will standing beside him as they waited for January and March.

Not only was the stepfather of all the brides acting as best man to all the bridegrooms, but the mother of the brides, having only recently been reconciled with her three daughters, was now about to give them all away to their future husbands.

It had been suggested by the three sisters, at a family get-together to discuss the wedding, that this role was much more suited to April than maid of honour, April obviously deeply touched by this honour from her three daughters.

April had married her David in a quiet ceremony the previous month—well, as quiet as it could have been when one of the newly married couple was an international film star, and the other an international film director, Jude recalled wryly.

But they had all been there, May acting as April's witness, Jude as David's, the eight of them disappearing off to a restaurant for a quiet meal to celebrate before the happy couple went off on a two-week honeymoon.

If anything, Jude's love and admiration for May had deepened during the last eight weeks, April's transition from film star into 'Mum' made all the easier for all the sisters because of May's obvious complete acceptance of her as such. The press, he had no doubts, would have a field day early next year once they realised that mother and daughter were appearing in a film together...

His heart began to beat faster as the playing of the church organ announced the arrival of the brides, a nerve pulsing in his jaw as he clenched his teeth together in anticipation.

'I've just seen May, Jude, so she hasn't changed her mind,' Max turned to softly tease him.

'They're *all* there, thank goodness,' Will added huskily after a brief nervous glance towards the back of the church.

Jude grinned at the two men. Strange, he had always

thought of these two men as close as brothers, and now they were about to become that in fact...

But all other thoughts fled his mind as he turned and saw May as she led the way down the aisle, a proud April at her side, the love shining in May's eyes echoed by the love in his own.

His own...

As he was May's.

Always.

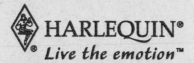

The world's bestselling romance series.

HARLEQUIN®
Presents~

Seduction and Passion Guaranteed!

MILLIONAIRE MARRIAGES

When the million-dollar question is "Will you marry me?"

**Coming Soon in Harlequin Presents...
An exciting duet by talented author**

Sandra Field

Don't miss...

**May 2004: The Millionaire's
Marriage Demand #2395**
Julie Renshaw is shocked when
Travis Strathern makes an
outrageous demand: marriage! She is
overwhelmingly attracted
to him—but is she ready to marry
him for convenience? Travis is used
to getting his own way—but Julie
makes certain he won't this
time...unless their marriage is based
on love as well as passion....

June 2004: The Tycoon's Virgin Bride #2401
One night Jenessa's secret infatuation with tycoon Bryce Laribee
turned to passion—but the moment he discovered she was a
virgin he walked out! Twelve years later, the attraction between
them is just as mind-blowing, and Bryce is determined to finish
what they started. But Jenessa has a secret or two....

Available wherever Harlequin books are sold.

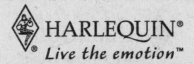

HARLEQUIN®
Live the emotion™

Visit us at www.eHarlequin.com

HPMILMAR

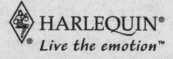

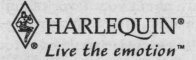

If you enjoyed what you just read,
then we've got an offer you can't resist!

Take 2 bestselling love stories FREE!

Plus get a FREE surprise gift!

Coming Next Month

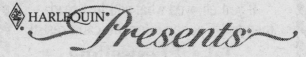

THE BEST HAS JUST GOTTEN BETTER!

#2397 THE SPANIARD'S BABY BARGAIN Helen Bianchin
Billionaire Manolo de Guardo has been dumped—by his nanny!
He needs someone to care for his daughter…fast! Ariane Celeste
is a Sydney reporter sent to interview him, and she's persuaded
to help out temporarily. But Manolo knows a good deal—and he
wants to keep Ariane….

#2398 THE PASSION PRICE Miranda Lee
When they were young Jake Winters walked out on Angelina, leaving her heartbroken and pregnant—and now he's back. Angelina is
amazed to see his transformation from bad boy
to sexy Sydney lawyer—and Jake is insistent that he will bed
Angelina one more time….

#2399 A SPANISH MARRIAGE Diana Hamilton
Javier married Zoe purely to protect her from male predators
who were tempted by her money and her beauty—he has all the
money he could ever need. But as their paper marriage continues
he finds it increasingly hard to resist his wife—even though he
made her a promise….

#2400 THE FORBIDDEN BRIDE Sara Craven
Zoe Lambert inherits a Greek island villa and sets off for a
new start in life. Her new home is perfect—and so is the sexy gardener who comes with it! But when Zoe discovers that Andreas
isn't just a gardener, but the wealthy son of a shipping tycoon, several startling events occur….

#2401 THE TYCOON'S VIRGIN BRIDE Sandra Field
One night Jenessa's secret infatuation with tycoon
Bryce Laribee turned to passion—but the moment he
discovered she was a virgin he walked out! Twelve years
later, the attraction between them is just as mind-blowing,
and Bryce is determined to finish what they started.

#2402 MISTRESS BY AGREEMENT Helen Brooks
From the moment tycoon Kingsley Ward walks into her office
Rosie recognizes the sexual invitation in his eyes. Kingsley's initial
purpose had been business, not pleasure. But Rosie is beautiful
and—unbelievably!—seems immune to his charms. Kingsley
decides he will pursue her….